SOCIETY

of the

SENTINELIA

SOCIETY
of the
SENTINELIA

Zahra of the Uwharries

Micki Bare

ISBN (Hardcover): 978-1-68512-125-9

First edition

ISBN: 978-1-68512-123-5

Cover art by Level Best Designs

This book was professionally typeset on Reedsy. Find out more at reedsy.com

To Elliott, Ethan, Evan, and Dave for your unwavering support and infinite love. You are my heart, my joy, and my inspiration always.

Contents

1

OUR TREE

Moss. I need one more kind of moss. My teacher Miss Evelie Poeley will be happy when she sees me walk into school with three kinds instead of two.

Father, Mother, and my sister Astrael are asleep, so I tip-toe out of our tree quieter than a bobcat waiting to pounce.

On my way out, I pass our neighbor's homes. When I get to Miss Evelie Poeley's doorway, my big toe slams into an acorn cap. My hands cover my ears. My eyes scrunch shut. With all the quiet around me, the cap bouncing off the wall sounds like a clap of thunder.

When I'm sure no one woke up, I creep to the knothole, look around to make sure I'm safe, and then glide out of our colony's tree. Miss Evelie Poeley says moss likes water, so I fly closer to the river. It's still dark and damp, but the sun will be up soon. I have to hurry.

Dew dots bright green bunches of fern leaves. Speckled gray rocks poke out of the ground. Just over a dead tree trunk covered in white lichen, I see something.

There it is! Puffy, light green moss. I land next to it. Some of it's bigger than me. Mounds grow tall on this smooth rock near the bottom of a tree. It's a whole moss colony! Careful not to crush any, I step between the heaps. Above me, the tree trunk groans in the wind. Bare branches sway. The sky is getting brighter.

GRUMMMM!

My hands fly up to my ears again. The noise. It's so loud. Worse than thunder. There's a horrible smell, too. I squat down in the moss. The grum sound won't stop. Then—

BRANG!

BRANG!

What's *that*? I keep my hands on my ears, but the noises are too loud. The grum doesn't stop and the brang clacks like a bird in danger. Only it's so much louder than a bird that my ears ache. I curl up in a ball and hide under my wings. I wish I stayed in bed. At home near Astrael. She'd make me feel better.

CRAAAACK!

The branging stops.

BAH-BOOOOM!

Everything shakes—the ground, trees, moss. The rock shivers.

There's a shrill scream. My eyes dart this way and that. It's me. *I'm* screaming!

I jump to my feet. I have to fly home. I push up through the air toward my colony. Before I get there I see them—big human machines. And humans. And . . .

"Mother! Father! Astrael!" I scream their names and then scream them again.

Our tree. Our colony. Our home. It's . . . all . . . smashed to the ground.

I squat on a branch and look all around. Where did they go?
I don't see any scraebins anywhere. Not one person from my
colony.

They must be nearby. I'll just wait. But I can't wait in this
tree. The humans might smash it down, too.

I hurry back to the moss and hide. And cry. What if . . .?

No! I shake my head. They're fine. They got out. They
just need to find me. There must be a safe place to wait. The
mossy mounds can't protect me from hawks or snakes or cats.
The bank of the river is better. My body shakes worse than a
leaf before a storm. Above me, a robin zooms by, followed by
another. As soon as they're both gone, I fly to the river.

Braided tree roots wind along the top of the bank in and out
of orange and brown mud on the walls of the river. I squat
down in the crook of a root to catch my breath. When I calm
down, I grab the root and stand to look back at the machines
and humans. From here, I can't see them. The grum and brang
still rumbles. The air is musty from the fallen tree. As I blink
away a tear, grimy, sweet smoke burns my eyes.

Something in the mud moves. I turn my head to look—

SPLASH!

That is much bigger than me. What is it?

The roots are now drenched and slippery. So are my hands
and feet. My foot slips off the crook.

I grab at the riverbank, but my hands sink into mud that
squishes through my fingers.

My other foot slips out from under me and my stomach
slams on a root hump.

Air. Knocked. Out.

Roots.

Mud.

Water.

Splashing and kicking and grabbing, flashes of water, mud, and trees tumble around me. The river pulls and pushes as it yanks me away.

Fly. I need to Fly.

THUD!

My back slams into a branch. I roll around, throw my arms over and hug as tightly as I can. My legs are too tired to climb. Instead, I slide one arm over, then the other. I do it again and again until my arms feel like they're going to snap.

Mud! My arm is touching the bank!

I grab and pull and yank until I'm wedged in a clump of laurel.

2

ZAHRA MEETS DANNI

The human girl sits cross-legged next to the river on a smooth gray speckled rock. She's twisting the end of one of her braids between her fingers. My neck feels hot and my hands shake. I'm afraid of humans. The first time I saw this one from the birdhouse, a chill bolted up my spine, and my throat dried up like an autumn leaf.

She's not as terrible as I expected. I've never seen her do anything bad. As she watches water lap against the rock and plays with her hair, she doesn't look like a scary creature.

But she *is* big.

Water sprays up and splatters her pants with dark spots. Those pants are going to be completely dark when the rain starts. I look up at the sky. Gray clouds will be here soon.

My frog-like feet—all screabins have legs and feet that resemble a frog, but we're not frogs—are periwinkle blue like the rest of my skin. They stick out against the brown and black decaying stump where I sit behind a dried up leaf. My brown top and tattered gray skirt—the same gray as the color of my hair—help hide me, but any moment now, the human is going to see my blue feet. I slide down the side of the stump and stand on soft, crumbly earth. There's a loblolly pinecone on the ground. I scoot behind it for cover. There's also a pin oak tree a few steps away with roots jutting into the river. I could hide there and then scurry back home.

No.

If I leave right now, she'd never know I was here. I need to meet her. I need her help.

SQUAWK!

Mr. Robin zooms through the yard and into the branches of the pin oak.

He followed me? I shake my head. Mrs. Robin joins her husband. They swoop between the human and me.

The girl's eyes lock onto mine.

I can't hear the river—just my pounding heart. I can't see the sky— only two giant green eyes staring into mine. Tingles burst through my spine like they did the day I first saw her next door.

Where are my words? I suck in a mouthful of air and push it past my twitching lips. "H-hello. My n-name is Zahra."

The girl doesn't move. The space between her round green eyes and my much smaller amethyst eyes is crushing my courage. Thoughts of my parents and sister flash through my mind. I can do this. I have to.

"Z-zahra. My name." I step away from the stump. My foot hits the pinecone, and it rolls away. "Zahra." My throat feels like it's full of sand.

The girl shoots up and loses her balance. She splashes into the river. Steadying herself with her hands on the rock, she snaps her head around and shouts, "Did you talk?"

My hands fly up to my ears. "You're so loud!"

Her face is squished like Father's when he tells stories about the brawl between Uncle Clay Aylward and a cat.

The river rushes past the human's knees, but she stands still. Without taking her eyes off me, she says in a softer voice, "My parents said North Carolina was going to be really different from New York, but this . . . you?" She points her chin at me. "What are you?"

North Carolina? New York? What does that mean? Mr. Robin swoops past the girl's head. I shake my head *no* at him. The girl ducks and swats at the air.

"Don't hurt him," I cry. "He's just protecting me."

She leans closer. "What?"

"The Robins. They're protecting me," I say in a louder voice.

"What? Those birds?" Her eyebrows scrunch. "What's going on? What are you?"

Mother and Father told Astrael and me over and over that only special adult humans know about scraebins. And only adult scraebins get to visit with those humans. I may be the youngest scraebin who ever talked to a human. I know I'm the only one to ever talk to a child human. Scraping together my last bits of courage, I put my sweaty hands on my hips and push back my shoulders. "I'm a scraebin."

"A scra . . . what?" Her eyes are squinty now.

"Scraebin," I repeat. I stomp my foot and stare.

"I've never heard of a scraebin. Is that even a real thing?" She rubs her eyes, blinks, looks up and down the river, and then at me.

My heart thumps against my ribs. My neck burns hot. "Yes, it's real." I point to my chest with my thumb. "*I'm* real!"

This is my first conversation with anyone since my family's home was destroyed. It's going all wrong. The days right after are a blur of shadows in my head. Somehow, I ended up in the Robins' birdhouse in the backyard next door to this human girl. They're birds. They chirp, sing, and sometimes squawk. But Mr. and Mrs. Robin don't talk. And I doubt they can help me find my family.

After climbing back onto the rock, the girl tells me her name is Danishia, but everyone calls her Danni. She leans on one foot, then the other. The Robins are still upset, but they finally go back to the birdhouse. From there, they keep screeching their danger call. Maybe it's time for me to go. I can always come back another day.

Danni wipes her hands across her pants, leaving orange mud streaks. Her eyes dart between the Robins and me. "Why haven't I ever seen a scraebin before? Are you from the zoo?" she asks.

Zoo? Where humans keep other creatures in cages? What an awful thing for her to say. I climb back to the top of the stump and try to come up with a quick answer. Not only are the Robins upset, but it's also about to rain. Dark clouds push away the white, puffy ones. "We stay hidden. Humans are big. And they like to dissect things," I explain. Then I turn to leave. I look up at the birdhouse.

She doesn't get the hint. "I suppose that's true." Danni cocks her head and then asks, "But if humans are dangerous, why did you come to *me*?"

This is my chance. It's why I'm here standing in front of a human. "Well, I ..." I want to tell her. I need to ask her for help, but it doesn't come out. And anyway, I really *do* need to get back. "I just thought since we were neighbors, I should say hello."

A plump, wet droplet bursts open on my head. Water slides

down my face and neck. I jump over to the pin oak and duck under a clump of dried leaves that refused to fall last autumn.

"Are you part frog and part fairy?" she asks, staring at my legs and ignoring the rain.

My hands curl into tight fists. "Did you really just call me a fairy?" I yell as I turn to look her right in those giant eyes. "I'm *not* a fairy. Fairies aren't real."

Her eyes get even bigger. She pulls on a braid. She cocks her head to one side. "But scraebins are?"

My eyes roll. I uncurl my fingers. Danni flings the damp braid out of her face and then crosses her arms. She asks if I can fly. Instead of telling the truth, I ask if she can fly. She squishes her face.

My wings are tucked away. After the fairy comment, I'm not about to let her know that scraebins actually *can* fly. By keeping it a secret, I have a way to escape if Danni puts me in danger. Even if my wings were out, she wouldn't be able to see them well, if at all. The color is not one humans can see. At least, that's what my teacher Miss Evelie Poeley says.

The Robins squawk again.

"I really should go." I step closer to the birdhouse. "The Robins are upset and it's raining."

"So, scraebins live with birds?"

My hands fly up to my cheeks and I shake my head. "No. I'm just living with them for now." I jump to the ground and grab a magnolia leaf for cover. Then I run to the birdhouse.

"I hope you'll come back," Danni yells.

After scrambling up the post, I pause at the door of the Robins' house. Danni is standing under her porch roof. She's staring at me. Water drips off her drenched braids.

Her relentless curiosity is exactly what I need—as long as

she isn't so curious that she decides to dissect me. Or send me to her zoo.

3

GLASS JARS

Rust-colored shorts and a green top lay across my bed, which is a nest of twigs, leaves, and moss Mrs. Robin made just for me. As soon as I climb to my loft, she gives me a nudge.

"Yes, Mrs. Robin. I'll put on my dry clothes. Thank you."

After I change, she pecks at the wet heap and moves the clothes to the highest part of the house. She puts my top and skirt over the skinny branch of a twig against the wall next to the round window. Then she hops down to the main floor and snuggles against Mr. Robin.

With the dark clouds and Mr. Robin blocking the door with his body, the birdhouse is dark. My eyes adjust as if I were in the tree where my family lived. I nibble a seed and then climb into bed.

All I can think about is my visit with Danni. When I close my eyes, her olive skin, thick dark braids, and full cheeks with deep dimples are as clear as if she were standing in front of me. She looked shocked when she first saw me. Then it looked like curiosity took over. I'm not sure if she'll help me or just want

11

to study me?

Everything I learned about humans from my teacher, Miss Evelie Poeley, drips back into my head like the drops of rain smacking the metal roof of the birdhouse. Humans are curious and need answers. They put other creatures into cages and study them. Sometimes, they put them on display in big glass tanks or, even worse, g l a s s … j a r s. Miss Evelie Poeley always stretched out the words like the sticky strands of a spider's web that sometimes get stuck between my foot and the ground. When she talked about it, she always looked sad.

My teacher said everyone in the forest knew a glass jar meant certain death. Lightning bugs got trapped in them. Frogs and salamanders, too. Humans give them food and water at first. But soon the glass jars are left alone. Forgotten. The creature starves, runs out of air or water, or gets too hot. No one hears its cries. No one rescues it. The creature suffers terribly. Then dies. Alone.

Remembering makes me wonder if Mother, Father, and Astrael ended up in glass jars? My heart races. I blink away a tear.

No! They're out there. Somewhere. They have to be. I just need to find them. I bury my face in my hands. My cheeks are wet. There must be a leak in the wall. I'll help the Robins fix it tomorrow.

* * *

Songs of nearby birds wake me. I wasn't sleeping well, anyway. Next to my nest are fresh sticks that look as if they were broken off a young tree. How sad for the tree. It must've hurt to have these pieces snapped off, but I need fresh sap to stay healthy.

The Robins somehow understand what I need, right up to gathering sticks each night while I sleep. I'm not sure how they know scraebins' wings have to absorb tree sap. When I find my colony and go back to school, I'll ask Miss Evelie Poeley.

My eyes are sore. The river is loud after the rain, rushing over rocks and logs. Drifting back to sleep would be easy, but my stomach grumbles. On the main floor, there are two dandelion buds and a raspberry blossom sitting on the flat piece of stone. The stone is my plate.

After breakfast, I lean the plate against the wall behind the Robins' nest. Then I go upstairs and fold my dry clothes. Mr. Robin is still sitting at the door. That can mean only one thing—I'm grounded. He's not going to let me go out to explore trees, swim in puddles, or collect flower petals. Another meeting with Danni isn't going to happen today, either.

That's okay. I'm too tired for any of that.

With my head resting against the wall, I look out the window. Branches with bright pink buds reach over the river. If I twist my neck just a bit, I can see Danni's rock. Two early spring butterflies flop around in the wind just above the stump.

Danni must be at her human school. Miss Evelie Poeley told us human children go to school in buildings with lots of rooms. I guess their colonies are too big for everyone to go to one teacher's main room for school. Danni probably has lots of human friends that laugh and play with her at school. Will she tell them about me?

One of the butterflies stops on top of a piece of grass. Its wings open and close. Open and close.

SLURP!

The tongue of a frog snaps out, long and quick, and the butterfly is gone. My hand slaps over my open mouth. I look away. That poor butterfly.

Such is nature, Mother always says. But I don't want to think about Mother right now. I go back to thinking about Danni. What if she tells a teacher about me? Grown-up humans are scarier than child humans. Would they tear down the birdhouse and put me in a glass jar? Or worse, cut me open, pull out my insides and study them? No wonder the Robins got upset when I went next door to meet her.

My eyes close. The air is fresh and cool from the rain. Sliding down the wall onto the floor, I lie on my back and let the sun warm my face.

When my eyes open, I see a line across the ceiling.

I crawl to the edge of the floor and look down. Mr. Robin isn't home. Mrs. Robin is propped at the door, facing outside. She's probably watching Mr. Robin gather worms and bugs. She's also blocking me from the door.

Standing straight up, my hands reach the line on the ceiling, so I push.

It opens!

Checking first to make sure Mrs. Robin didn't notice, I prop the ceiling door open with my elbow. There's a whole other room up here. An attic.

It's dark and empty. As my eyes adjust, I see streaks on the floor. Leaning down, I swipe my hand across one. It's sticky like dried sap. This must be where the Robins keep my sticks. There aren't any sticks here, now. Maybe Mr. Robin is out collecting more.

A sliver of sunlight cuts down one slope of the metal roof. Another door? It easily opens with a gentle nudge. My eyes feel like giant petals opening with the morning sun. Not only can I see the river and Danni's rock, but also her entire backyard.

Mr. Robin flies past. I duck and the roof slams shut!
With my heart pounding louder than a human car thundering by, I scurry to my nest.

4

THE OBSERVATORY

When Danni gets home from school, I scramble back up to my attic observatory and push it open with both hands. Spending time up here connects me to the trees, river, and grass. I don't mind being grounded when I'm in my observatory. Except when I think of the frog eating the butterfly for lunch. *Bleech!*

I push that vision out of my head and watch Danni. Instead of going straight to her glass-topped table with her books the way she always does after school, she walks to the edge of her backyard. She looks at the birdhouse, then all around the yard, and then back in my direction.

I freeze. My hands shake.

She'll notice the movement if the roof closes. So instead, I stay as still as a scared possum. The roof isn't open enough for someone of Danni's size to notice any difference. At least, that's what I hope. If the Robins weren't keeping me inside, I'd open the roof wide, wave, and call out to her, *"Danni, I'm here! Wait and I'll come down!"*

But if I say that now, she'll come to the birdhouse. The

Robins will go berserk. Then I'd be grounded forever.

Danni stares in my direction and squints. My muscles feel like rocks. She cocks her head and stares into the space between her yard and my house. She looks at the log cabin behind my house. Finally, she goes to her table and opens books. My arms relax. I push the stick back in its place and watch.

When she finishes her schoolwork, she walks to the stump where I stood the day before. She's carrying a pencil and a book. She looks all around the stump and tree. Can she tell that's where a butterfly became a frog's lunch? She moves dried leaves and brushes away dirt. She picks up the pinecone I hid behind. After looking at it, she drops the pinecone and writes in the book. Finally, she puts the pencil and book in her pocket. She picks up a long stick and sits cross-legged on her rock, poking at the water. She looks in my direction. She pokes the water again.

She looks sad. And lonely. The way her face looks matches how I feel most days. It was how I felt this morning. But now, in my observatory, I feel happy. Except when I remember that frog. But all creatures must live and die according to nature. Mother said so when I was little and cried when the purple flowers near our tree dried up and died.

While Danni sits and pokes at the river, I look around her yard. Be aware of what's around you, Father always reminds us. A blue tube is curled up like a snake next to the house. Wasps—or maybe they're yellow jackets—buzz around plants that spill down the sides of two orange pots on either side of the covered porch. The black grill where her father sometimes cooks food stands out like a buzzard cutting through a blue sky to dive after what's left of a dead rabbit.

17

There's a patch of dirt near the river and another next to her other neighbor. Both have bright white rocks around them. The grass between the porch and the river is mostly brown and yellow, but there are a few clumps of bright green. Tall seed shoots wobble in the breeze. Nothing dangerous. And in all the time I've spent watching her, I never saw Danni holding a glass jar.

She pokes at the river until her mother calls her for supper. Once Danni's inside, I pull the stick away and close the roof. In the main room, two blackberries and a small pile of seedpods sit on my plate. Mr. Robin knows the seedpods are my favorite.

"Thank you," I say.

He chirps as if he understands and is replying, *"My pleasure."*

The Robins eat worms for supper. It's an awful sight. I know birds eat worms and crickets and bugs of all sorts, but I don't like to watch. Head down, I stare at my own food. On days it's too awful, I take my plate to my loft and eat alone.

I don't like to eat alone.

Pressing the seedpods between two fingers the way Father taught me, I push out the seeds. Father always picked the best seedpods. He loves to gather food and prepare meals with Mother. He hums when he cooks. Sometimes, Father asks Astrael and me to taste a new recipe of berries and petals or nuts and seeds. When we like it, he makes up a song to remember how to make it next time. When we scrunch our faces, he sets it outside for birds and squirrels to eat. Then he and Mother make one of our favorite suppers instead.

I pick at a blackberry, but I'm not hungry. The leftover seedpods go next to the wall. Mr. Robin finishes the blackberries. Those are his favorite even if he does eat lots of worms. Mrs. Robin brushes her wing across my arm as I wipe off my plate.

It's good they protect me, but I need them to stop grounding me. I *have* to see Danni again. She has to help me.

5

THE KNOTHOLE

A clap of thunder jolts me awake.

Outside, the sky is gray. Mist makes my hand wet when I stretch it out the door. Below the birdhouse, Mr. Robin hops around catching food. Mrs. Robin weaves blades of dry grass into her nest.

While waiting for breakfast, I crawl to my room. No sappy stick today. The weather must've kept the Robins from being able to bring one home last night. Maybe they'll let me go outside after breakfast.

Way above the ground, much higher than our birdhouse, the pin oak by Danni's rock has a large knothole. The day I woke up confused and couldn't remember how I ended up in a birdhouse, that knothole was the first thing I noticed—probably because I needed it.

When I was strong enough, it was where I had to go. During that first visit, I'd hoped to find my family. My heart thumped so hard it felt loud enough to wake a bear out of hibernation. Inside, I found a deep tunnel with sappy walls. It was definitely big enough for my parents and sister. When I breathed in, a shiver crawled up my spine and made the hairs on my neck pop out. It smelled just like home.

Mother? Father? Astrael?

No one was there. The knothole was as empty as my heart. But my body needed the sap, so I explored. Each visit after that first, I learned more about its rooms and passageways. It would be a great place to live. Scraebins *do* need to live in trees. But being there alone makes me sad.

After breakfast, I point to the tree and then to the floor under my feet, "May I go to the pin oak? I'll come straight back."

Mr. Robin looks at Mrs. Robin, at me, and then at Mrs. Robin again. He steps closer to the door. Mrs. Robin looks only at me. Then she nudges me outside.

My dorsal wings—the ones I use to fly—slide out from underneath my collarbones. My pectoral wings—the ones that both steady and camouflage me—extend and then wrap around the front of my body. From the edge of the birdhouse, I push myself into the wind.

The added weight of the misty droplets makes my body feel heavy. Every flap of my wings is harder than the last.

I panic and push harder.

It takes all my strength to clear the distance between the birdhouse and the tree. When I finally make it, I land far below the big knothole. I'm damp from mist and sweat. On the side of the tree, my toes curl into the bark. My fingers grab hold of the tree, but I can't climb.

I have to rest. Catch my breath.

The knothole is too high up to see. Why am I so weak? I slept just fine curled next to Mrs. Robin. I woke up tired, but after I ate, I felt okay. This doesn't make sense.

Mrs. Robin dives from the birdhouse and swoops to the

underside of a thin branch low on the trunk. She's upside down, clutching the twig with her talons. She looks down at me and chirps. Her claws move from side to side gripping, letting go, and gripping again. Her head darts this way and that with each chirp. She sounds worried. I feel worried. I know I have to climb.

My hands shake. My feet feel like they've been buried by a mudslide. Step by step, I make my way to the thin branch. Mrs. Robin flips right side up and flies up to a higher, thicker branch. It's near a small knothole.

"Good idea, Mrs. Robin," I say as I pant. My lips and tongue are dry.

The smaller knothole. That's my new goal. But first, I need to rest again.

Mrs. Robin keeps chirping, pushing me to climb. I stop again with my belly against the tree and my eyes closed.

I need. To catch. My. Breath.

The sun is high and the mist gone when I crawl into the knothole. The only clouds left are thin streaks. The space is just big enough for me and maybe one other if we didn't mind scrunching close together. It isn't tall enough to stand. But then, I'm too tired to stand. I pull my knees to my chest and wrap my hands around my legs.

Keeping my wings out just a bit, I let the sap work. My eyes close. I imagine bringing Astrael here one day. I imagine us sitting close together, cozy and warm, while she tells me stories. My breaths grow long. And deep.

"Zahra? Are you here? Zahra?"

"Mother?" I whisper as my eyes flutter open.

6

DANNI'S BAD DAY

"Do you really exist, Zahra?"

Blinking away dreams of my family, my heart sinks. Tears cloud my eyes. Danni, not my mother, stands next to the pin oak, looking at the birdhouse. Mrs. Robin is perched at her front door, watching Danni, but staying silent. My wings curl around my body. Danni sits down and leans against the tree. I scoot farther inside the knothole. Then I rest my head on my elbow at the edge.

"I wish you'd come out again, Zahra," she begins, holding her face in her hands and resting her elbows on her knees. "I really need a friend. The girls at school are so . . . so . . ."

Her voice trails off beneath an avalanche of sniffles. She's crying. My own tears drip onto the rim of the knothole.

Finish your sentence. What's wrong with the girls at school? I swipe my sleeve across my face.

"I bet you wouldn't care I look different from my parents or that we all have a weird northern accent." *Sniffle*. "Why do they have to call me 'brainiac' just because I do well on tests and do my homework?" *Sniffle. Sniffle.* "Is it so weird to like

23

learning new things?" *Sniffle.*

The humans at Danni's school sound awful.

She drops her face in her hands again. "What will they say when I get my new glasses?" She sobs. Then, after a long sigh, she wipes her face with her hands and pulls a dark, shiny rectangle thing from her pocket. She taps and it lights up. It's so pretty. She taps and touches. Lights and colors dance as her fingers move. I lean out for a closer look.

"Danni! Time to eat!" I look at Danni's house. An adult human with skin the color of sand and long, wavy hair as orange as yam flesh stands in the doorway.

"Coming!" Danni yells back.

My hands clap over my ears. Danni walks to her house and disappears inside.

The sun is nearly gone. I wasn't going to spend this much time in the knothole. The Robins won't be happy.

My wings feel strong enough to fly. Mrs. Robin lands on a branch beside the knothole. She chirps sharply.

"I'm sorry I stayed so long. And I didn't know Danni was going to come out and sit by this tree."

Mrs. Robin shakes her head and chirps again. I look all around—from the river to the log cabin house in our yard, around Danni's yard, at the clumps of overgrown grass, and all around the birdhouse—to make sure there aren't any humans nearby. The way Mrs. Robin's chirping, the path home must be clear. There are plenty of lightning bugs out, as well. It must be safe to travel.

As soon as I step out of the knothole, Mrs. Robin flies to the birdhouse. I stop and remember my earlier journey. With my eyes on the birdhouse, I push away from the knothole. My body sails into the air. The cool breeze rushes over my face and through my hair. Mrs. Robin is barely inside when I land at the door.

That's how flying is supposed to feel!

Mr. Robin sits next to the food that's already set out for supper. Mrs. Robin settles next to him. I take my usual spot. More seeds and two blackberries. It looks delicious, but I can't eat a bite. It's terrible to leave it all on my plate, but I'm not a bit hungry. My body feels so much better than this morning, but my feelings are like a storm swirling with heavy rain, zaps of lightning, and claps of thunder.

Danni's voice echoes in the storm. I ached to reach out when she was crying, but with Mrs. Robin watching and my doubts about humans, I was too scared.

What was that shiny thing that lit up when she touched it? Could she be magical, like a witch or elf? Astrael used to tell me stories about humans that had special powers, but she promised the stories were made-up, like the tales of woodland fairies and unicorns. She said witches were also pretend. And elves, too. Nope, I'm not going to be able to eat tonight.

"You can have the berries," I say as I slide them toward Mr. Robin. Then I go up to my nest and wait for them to fall asleep.

7

HEART STRINGS

The crackling of twigs rubbing together every time I move has to be keeping the Robins awake. When the moon reaches its highest point, I creep to the attic and push the roof open.

"I bet you wouldn't care I look different from my parents or that we all have a weird northern accent."

Danni's words repeat in my head. Why do other human kids at school care that she doesn't have the same color hair as her parents? Or that she has olive skin and her mom has skin like sand? And what's a weird northern accent?

"Why do they have to call me 'brainiac' just because I do well on tests and do my homework? Is it so weird to like learning new things?"

It's wonderful to learn new things. Don't all humans want to do well in school? Scraebins do. School is fun. *Was* fun. I miss school so much. I miss Miss Evelie Poeley.

"What will they say when I get my new glasses?"

What are glasses? My eyes open wide and my heart pounds. Do new glasses mean she's bringing home glass jars?

To try to make sense of it all, I dig into my feelings. My heart feels Danni's sadness. And even though she's getting "new glasses," which may or may not be about glass jars, I still want to talk to her again and learn more.

Her voice made me curious, not scared. When she began to cry, I cried. I didn't want to hide. I wanted to stroke her hair like Astrael always does when I'm sad.

My sister told me our hearts talk to us. When there's danger, our hearts scream at us to get away. When there is love and kindness, our hearts weave invisible strings that connect us. When love and kindness grow, the invisible strings become stronger than a raging river after days of rain.

When the strings break—like the day our house was destroyed, separating me from my family—the pain is sharp and heavy.

Sitting on the floor of my observatory, I squeeze my eyes to push the tears back. My family is out there somewhere. My heart says so. The strings connecting us are still there. I feel them through the sadness and pain.

Listening to nighttime sounds helps break up the storm in my mind. Crickets chirping. Water babbling. Leaves rustling. The hoot of an owl. When the urge to cry goes away, I look out at the moonlit world. Is my heart saying my family is out there? Yes. Is my heart saying Danni can help me find them? Yes. The cool breeze hits my face. The moon reflects off the white feathers of an owl that sits high in a tree. A cricket bounces from a blade of grass and lands on a clump of dirt.

SNAP!

My heart races. I turn in the direction of the sound. It's that old lady human! She's walking from the log cabin to the birdhouse. *My* birdhouse!

The creek of the roof as I close it sounds louder to me now than Mr. Robin's squawk. Back in my nest, I squish my ear to the wall and listen.

The old lady's footsteps get louder. Then they stop. There's no sound at all. She must be right next to the birdhouse. Had she seen me? My wings wrap around my body.

The roof creaks. She's opening it!

There's no way she can get to me. If she puts her giant human hand through the roof, she can touch the attic and maybe reach the top floor. But she'd have to have arms made of fresh blades of grass to reach me on the middle floor. If she tries the front door, Mr. and Mrs. Robin will peck until her arms bleed.

I'm safe. I'm safe. I'm safe.

She must've seen the roof when I had it open. She's curious. She probably wonders how Mr. and Mrs. Robin opened it.

There's more creaking. The roof slaps closed.

CLOMP! CLOMP! CLOMP!

The footsteps move away. She's walking back to the log cabin. I let out a big sigh. She's gone.

Father's words pop back into my head. He always tells us to "be aware" and make sure there are no humans around when we go outside. We never saw humans where we lived.

Now, they surround me.

8

NO SECRETS

M r. Robin caught me looking at him from under the roof shingle, so he flew back home. Now he stands in my loft chirping for me to come down. Mrs. Robin, who already knew about my observatory, nudges him down to the main floor. She then looks up and nods.

"Thank you," I say. Then I close the hatch and sit down on the rock I use as a seat. A blanket Mrs. Robin made for me is on the floor. It has pink and violet petals and honey-yellow strips of tossasides—things humans leave on the ground.

Looking out, I see danger lurking in the grass. A baby cat is wandering around the yard. It isn't much bigger than me. Its fur is fluffy and gray. But not stormy dark gray like my hair. It's more like the clouds after it stops raining. Its eyes are bright amethyst—*exactly* like mine. It creeps through the overgrown grass between the river and the birdhouse.

Danni immediately spots the cat when she gets home from school. "Oh! A kitten. It's so cute."

Sun bounces off her face, creating dark spots everywhere I look. After a few blinks, the spots disappear. On her nose sit spectacles. Spectacles? Of course! When she said she was getting glasses, what she meant was spectacles. And spectacles are nothing like glass jars.

Danni walks closer and pulls the shiny black thing out of her pocket. She holds it in front of the cat, which is now standing still. Was she going to cast a spell? No. Magic isn't real.

CLICK!

The cat bolts toward the river and disappears. Danni slides her shiny thing back into her pocket.

"Zahra, I'm glad you said hello to me that day." She pushes her spectacles up her nose.

I close the roof so she doesn't hear it. Then I hop down to the front door to peek out.

"I'm a really nice person, but I understand if you're scared because I'm too big," Danni hangs her head. "And a human." She turns to walk away.

Mrs. Robin nudges me closer to the door. I whisper, "Should I call her?" Mrs. Robin's eyes grow big. She nudges me again. Mr. Robin chirps. A grin spreads across my face. "Danni! Wait!"

Her head flies around, followed by the rest of her body. "Zahra?"

My shoulders scrunch up to my ears. Her voice is loud and sharp.

"How are you?" she asks with a quieter voice. As she steps closer, her smile droops. "Are you all right?"

"Yes," I tell her. "Why?"

"You look," Danni starts. She cocks her head to one side. "You look pinkish. I thought your skin was bluer?"

"Periwinkle blue, yes," I reply. But she's right. My arms and legs are *pinkish*, as she put it. "When I get sick, my skin turns amaranth. But I didn't think I was feeling bad enough for it to flush amaranth again."

"Amaranth? Again?"

I roll my eyes. "Pinkish. Yes. I had a bad spell yesterday."

"Are you well enough now to come with me to the rock?"

I look at the Robins. They don't step closer to the doorway or squawk. "I think so."

Danni steps closer.

"Wait!" I blurt out as my hand flies up between Danni and me. "What's that black shiny thing you keep in your pocket? And how do you make it light up? Are you . . . magic?" It's silly to ask, but it's also best to make sure.

Danni laughs and then answers, "No, I'm not magic. That's just my phone."

"Your phone?" Miss Evelie Peoley told us human phone machines were as big as a skunk's tail. Too big to fit in a pocket. "But you pointed it at the cat."

"I was taking a picture," she says, like *that* makes perfect sense. Which it does not.

My shoulders shrug, and my hand drops to my side. "But I thought humans used cameras to take pictures."

"We do," she says. "My phone is also a camera. Let's go sit on the rock. I'll show you what else it can do. I can carry you if you like." She reaches her hands up to the door of the birdhouse.

A tingly feeling spreads from my legs and arms to my toes and fingers. The Robins are right here if I need them. And I can always fly away. After a quick glance, I know the old lady isn't outside. There are no other humans in the area.

"Okay," I finally answer.

She leaves her hands open as she carries me to her rock. She's extra careful, as if I'm a bird egg and will shatter if she drops me. She doesn't want to hurt me. The tingly feeling is gone by the time we get to her rock. Danni bends over so I can step down. Then she sits next to me.

"Thank you for coming out today," she says, looking at the river instead of me.

"I'm sorry your friends don't like your spectacles. I think they're pretty."

"My spectacles?" Danni questions. Then she touches them. "Oh, my glasses. Thank you. And they're not my friends. I don't have friends at school."

I get up and walk between her and the river. "That's awful! I don't understand how that could be possible." I put my hands on my hips. "If I were a human, I'd want to be your friend."

Danni moves her eyes from the river to me. "Thank you, Zahra." She takes her phone out and shows me the picture she took of the cat. It's even scarier in the photo. While she's still holding up the cat picture, she asks, "Can I ask you something?"

"Yes, please do."

"Why do you live with birds?"

My head drops. I stare at the rock. No crying. Not now. Big. Deep. Breath. "I left home early one day, before the sun was up. I was collecting moss. We were learning about it in school."

"I love science, too," Danni says. She grins.

I'm not smiling.

Her grin disappears. "I'm sorry I interrupted. Go ahead."

"There were two kinds of moss near home, but I wanted to find something different. So I kept searching and walking farther and farther away. Then, when the sun was just above the horizon, I heard an awful noise." No tears. I sniffle. "I tried to get back home, but there were big machines and humans everywhere." The tears fall. Stupid tears.

"I'm so sorry," Danni says. She brushes her finger against my shoulder. The tingly feeling strikes like a bolt of lightning. "That must've been terrible. What happened?"

I rub my shoulder, sniffle, and then try to answer. "I don't know. My parents, my sister Astrael, our friends and neighbors, our entire colony . . . were just gone. The tree. Our homes. Everything. All gone."

Danni pulls a soft, flimsy piece of paper out of her pocket, tears off a piece, and then hands it to me. "What did you do?"

I take the paper handkerchief and blow my nose. "I cried. A lot. And I hid in the banks of the river."

"What river?" Danni looks around.

"This one," I say as I point to the water.

Danni shakes her head. "This isn't a river. It's a stream." She taps her phone, and then holds it out the way she did with the cat picture. "*This* is a river."

After wiping my nose again, I look at her phone. Wow! It's not a picture. It's like a real river trapped inside her phone! And trees and birds and a bright blue sky.

"Maybe I can help you find your family," Danni says.

The words knock me off balance. I grab hold of the phone so I don't fall. My body gets warm all over. Danni's going to help me find Mother, Father, and Astrael!

The next day, as soon as Danni closes her school books, I scramble down from my observatory and listen for her voice.

"May I help you?" I stop short in the middle of the birdhouse. The voice is *not* Danni's.

33

9

THE OLD LADY

There's another human outside with Danni. We're supposed to make a plan to find my family, but I can't let somebody else see me.

"Hello, ma'am. How are you, today?" Danni says. She sounds different.

"What are you doing in my backyard?" The other voice cackles.

The old lady human who lives in the log cabin is standing between Danni and the birdhouse. My legs, arms, and neck burn. Please, Danni, please don't tell the old lady human about me.

"I . . . I, uhm," Danni sputters.

"Well? Don't you have your own backyard?" she asks Danni. Then she looks up at the sky and shakes her head. "Remember when our house was the only one for miles?"

Danni looks up.

The old lady human squints at Danni. "Well? Don't you?"

Danni looks at her. "Yes, ma'am. I'm sorry. I didn't think you'd mind."

"Mind what? What are you doing here?"

"You have a beautiful birdhouse, and, I . . . uhm . . ."

No Danni! Don't tell her about me.

"I like nature. And science. The robins in your birdhouse are fascinating. We've been studying birds at school. And. Well. I don't have a birdhouse in *my* yard." She still sounds different as she chokes out her answers.

Then Danni looks right at me. When the old lady human follows her eyes and turns, I jerk out of sight. As I slide down and sit with my back against the wall, relief covers me like Mrs. Robin's blanket. Danni didn't tell her about me. Danni *is* a human I can trust.

"Well, I do have a nice backyard," the old lady human replies. "We did keep it nice, didn't we, Herbert?" Then she warns Danni, "But it's not safe for children."

"Not safe? Why?" Now that's Danni's *real* voice. It's nice to hear her sound like her again. And it's an excellent question. I look out.

"The crook in the stream right there," the old lady human points to where the bank curves in and then back out. "It's full of snakes. And not the good kind that keep varmints away. The bad, poisonous kind that can kill you in minutes.

"I'm an old woman. I can't keep all the poison ivy out of the yard. It's growing everywhere. You're bound to end up in the hospital all swollen from rash. And they'd have to give you shots with big needles to make you well again." She winks at the sky and then points to Danni's house. "So, you scamper back to your yard and stay there."

Danni hangs her head and replies, "Yes, ma'am." Then she turns and walks away.

"If you come back, I'll have to tell your parents." She watches

Danni walk to the table, gather her books, and then go inside. Then she turns around. I duck. "Herbert, it's just awful the way things have gotten. Children wander about unsupervised. More houses are being built every day. It's such a different world. And I'm getting old. And tired." Her voice is gruff like the grunt of angry deer except when she's talking to someone she calls Herbert. He must either be invisible or so far up in the sky that he can't be seen by a scraebin.

When the log cabin door closes, I poke my head out and look around. There's no poison ivy in her yard. None of the snakes I've seen are poisonous. The only threats around here are an owl that has no interest in humans and a puffy gray cat.

10

THE GRAY CAT

"Here kitty, I have a treat for you."

Danni squats down at the edge of the grass, careful not to step into the old lady human's backyard.

If that cat was not lurking about, I would've been waiting for her on the rock. Walking is out of the question around cats. Also, unlike humans, cats can see scraebins' wings. They like to chase creatures that fly, like birds, butterflies, and especially scraebins. And cats climb trees.

All day, that gray fluffy ball wandered between our houses. When it couldn't catch a brown and blue butterfly, I thought it might give up and go back to the river. Well, "stream" according to Danni. My plan was to dash out as soon as the cat was gone.

It never left.

Now Danni's calling out to the one thing that stands in the way of a plan to find my parents. She has something wet in her hand. She waves the pink blob back and forth making the air stink. That cat doesn't want to eat human food. What's Danni thinking?

The cat walks toward her.

"Oh, look at you. You're beautiful. And you have purple eyes, just like Zahra." She jiggles her hand again. "Here you go. It's salmon. I bet you'll like it."

The cat walks closer, stopping every few steps. Its back is arched. That can only mean one thing—it's going to attack Danni! I have to help her, but how?

The old lady human must be inside. No other humans or animals are in sight. My wings begin to extend. Mr. Robin lands on the perch just outside the birdhouse door. He chirps and then hops inside, blocking my path. I retract my wings.

"That's it. Come on, little one," Danni continues.

"Danni!" I try to yell a warning. It's barely a whisper. It feels like there's a clump of mud and leaves halfway between my stomach and the back of my tongue. I want to look away, but I can't.

The cat jumps close to Danni, grabs the food, and then bolts away. But it doesn't go far. It drops the pink blob of salmon, sniffs it, and then nibbles. I slump to the floor. That was close. Grabbing the side of the doorway, I push my head past Mr. Robin.

"If you liked that, I have plenty more," Danni calls to the cat.

Again? Why won't she leave it alone?

She pulls out another piece. The cat walks back to Danni and takes it. This time, the cat's back isn't arched. It doesn't bolt away. Instead, it eats the smelly blob and rubs its body across Danni's leg.

She gives the cat another large piece and rubs her hand on its head. My hands begin to sweat.

"You're such a sweet kitty. I think we'll be great friends."

Friends? Now she wants to be friends with the cat? What about helping me find my family? Then I remember. That old lady human scared Danni away.

She rubs the cat's head one more time. After she picks up the can, she disappears inside her house.

Mr. Robin flies away, probably to get more bugs or berries. I suck in a deep breath. As the air drifts back out, a chill sweeps through my body. The gray cat created a problem. The blanket in the observatory is warm. I need time to think. And watch.

The cat walks over to Danni's door, curls up on the doormat, and then falls asleep. It looks comfortable. My hand balls up. This purple-eyed varmint will *not* steal my friend and interfere with our plans. There has to be a way to meet with Danni again. I need time to explain the dangers of cats. Once that cat is gone, we can work together to find my family.

11

PETS

The next day, the cat is nowhere in sight. Right after lunch, I fly over to the pin oak and sit against the trunk on the first branch. When Danni gets home from school and sits on her rock, I hop down.

"Zahra! I knew you'd come here after Mrs. Erdos banned me from her yard."

"Mrs. Erdos?" I ask.

"Yes, the lady who lives in the log cabin. Her name is Mildred Erdos."

It's good to know the name of the person who chased away Danni. Mrs. Mildred Erdos and a gray cat—the list of creatures to avoid keeps growing. That reminds me, I have to ask, "Have you seen that cat, today?"

"Not today. You know, she's only a kitten. A baby. She's alone and scared. We need to be nice to her."

Clearly, no one in Danni's life has ever been attacked by a cat. When Aunt Lily Aylward was alive, all she ever talked about was how Uncle Clay Aylward injured his wing in a brawl with a ferocious orange and white cat. He was never able to fly again, which meant they stayed home all the time.

"Cats are mean and dangerous. I just don't want you to get hurt," I tell her.

Danni giggles. "Humans keep cats as pets. They're snuggly and warm. They comfort us when we don't feel well. And they keep the mice and—" Her smile goes away. She cocks her head and pushes up her spectacles. "What's wrong?"

"You capture cats? You keep them captive?" The muddy leaf knot from my throat reappears in the pit of my stomach.

"Captive? Well, no, not really. Don't screabins have pets?"

My head drops. "No." I need Danni's help, but I don't want to be her pet.

"Why not?" she asks. "Pets are our friends."

"I suppose," I try to agree. Then I explain, "We just don't do that. We'd never take an animal away from its family just so it could be friends with us."

"I'm sorry, Zahra. I didn't mean to hurt your feelings. Humans are just different, I guess. And I always thought cats and dogs liked being part of our families."

I look up at Danni. "Do you have pets?" What if she has a dog? Or another cat?

"No. My parents both work. They think having pets would be a—" Danni makes her voice low and rolls her eyes, "commitment we're just not ready to make."

That's a relief. "So, they won't let you keep that cat?"

"Why don't you like cats?" Danni pauses a moment. "Do cats attack screabins?"

Surprised she even has to ask, I answer, "Sometimes."

"That's awful. I promise, I won't let this kitten hurt you," she says, shaking her head.

"Thank you, but maybe if you just leave it alone, it'll go away for good. Then we won't have to worry about it."

Danni shrugs off my suggestion. She leans in and looks at me. "Are you okay, Zahra? You still look pink. And you have bags under your eyes."

"I know. I'll be okay. It's just that I live in a birdhouse instead of a tree."

Danni looks at the birdhouse, then cocks her head and looks at me. "The birdhouse makes you sick?" Danni's eyes and nose wrinkle.

"Not the birdhouse exactly." It takes me a second to figure out how to answer. "Scraebins need tree sap. It keeps our . . . I mean . . . we need it to stay healthy." She still doesn't know about my wings. Until this cat situation is sorted, it's a fact I need to keep to myself.

"You need to *drink* sap? Like syrup?"

Drink syrup? It's sweet and sticky. It'd be gross to swallow. "No, we don't drink it. Our bodies absorb nutrients from the sap."

"That's so cool!" Danni blurts out. Then her eyes grow big. "Oh, but you aren't getting sap in the birdhouse."

"Sometimes I get a little when the Robins bring up fresh sticks. And sometimes I take naps in the knothole in this tree." I point to the pin oak. "But with that cat lurking around, I haven't had a chance to get up there."

"If Mrs. Erdos wasn't so worried about me being in her yard, I'd carry you to the tree. If you go there every day, you'll feel better," Danni offers.

How rude! "Won't your parents be upset if you keep calling Mrs. Mildred Erdos just 'Mrs. Erdos'?"

Danni shakes her head. "No. Why?"

"My parents would be upset. I was taught we must always

address elders by their title, first name, and last name. It's just respectful," I explain.

"I suppose humans aren't that formal, but we're still respectful."

I'm not sure I understand, but Danni doesn't act like there's a problem. Instead, her eyebrows fly up. "I've got a great idea! Why don't you move into the knothole in this tree over here?" She points to the old pecan tree near her house. It has a branch that stretches almost to a window on the second level of her house. She follows my eyes. "That's my bedroom."

"Move?" I ask. I feel alone enough as the only screabin in the Robins' birdhouse. But at least they look after me. And feed me. "I don't know." I look down at my feet. All I see is amaranth.

"There's got to be a way I can help," Danni says.

"What I really want is for you to help me find my family."

"Of course. That's what I want, too. But until we do, I think it might be healthier for you to move into a tree. I'll bring you lots of food. And I'll watch over you." Danni's eyes are wide as she babbles out ideas. "What do you like to eat? My mom sometimes makes spaghetti with her own meat sauce. And we eat take-out food a lot. Do you like Chinese food?"

Humans probably don't eat grass seedpods. Or apple blossoms. And certainly not blackberry pecan stew. That's one of my favorites.

After Danni leaves for supper, I climb the pin oak all the way to the large knothole. Not only does it have the most sap, it's out of sight of cats and humans. When the lightning bugs start to blink, I know it's time to head home.

In front of the birdhouse, Mr. Robin swoops and chirps. A quick glance around both backyards tells me there are no humans, cats, or other predators. With my wings outstretched, I step out of the knothole.

The air is heavy. The birdhouse isn't getting closer. The ground *is*.

I'm not strong enough to fly? I'm not strong enough to fly!

12

CAT ENCOUNTER

My heart beats so fast it feels like it might jump out of my mouth.

THUMP!

I plop down in a soft patch of overgrown grass and moss. I lift my head and look around. The tree is much closer than the birdhouse. Mrs. Mildred Erdos is on her porch eating a sandwich. She's looking this way. How did I miss seeing her from the tree?

Shaking my head in disappointment, I slump down to rest and think. A branch must've blocked my view of her porch.

Mrs. Mildred Erdos is old, so maybe her eyes are too weak to see me this far away. If I move close to the stream, the grass should be tall enough to hide me. I'll take my time and save energy so I can climb the post when I get to the birdhouse.

Before taking a step, I see the baby cat out of the corner of my eye.

I freeze.

My heart thumps and thumps and thumps so fast. I wish Danni was still outside.

The cat creeps closer. My eyes fill with tears. I don't want to die. I want Father. He'd know what to do.

The cat stops. It looks directly into my eyes. My shoulders shake with the chill.

Then I see it. Danni was right—its eyes are the same exact shade of amethyst as mine.

Its back isn't arched.

After my heart calms, the cat takes another step. I suck in the damp air. The cat steps again. When it's close enough that I could reach out and touch it if I wanted to touch a cat, it makes a rumbling hum noise. Mr. and Mrs. Robin circle back and forth between the birdhouse and me, but I don't look up. I can't take my eyes off the cat.

It sits down right in front of me. The rumbling continues. It reaches its paw out and brushes my leg. A spark of panic shoots up my back.

"Please, cat. Please let me go."

There is scuffling on the porch. I look up and see Mrs. Mildred Erdos. She stands at the rail and looks this way. Will she shoo the cat away? Does she see me?

The cat reaches its paw out again, but this time it nudges me. I look into its eyes and whisper, "What are you doing? What do you want?" I look at Mrs. Mildred Erdos and then back at the cat. My courage grows. I am, after all, talking to a cat. Aunt Lily Aylward and Uncle Clay Aylward would fall down with heart attacks if they saw this. Well, if they weren't already dead.

The cat nudges me again. Then it dips its head low to the ground. I breathe in a gulp of air. What does my heart say? I breathe out. I don't sense danger.

"Climb on your back?" I ask, as if it could answer.

But it does. The cat says yes with a quiet meow.

Mrs. Mildred Erdos puts her plate on the rail and walks to the steps. This odd cat is my only chance of getting back to the birdhouse without being caught by a human.

After sucking in another long, deep breath, I climb onto the cat's back and grab its scruff. My wings curl around my body to hide me from Mrs. Mildred Erdos. The cat trots toward the birdhouse, moving faster with each step. When we get to the post, Mr. Robin lets out a horrible squawk.

Birds fear cats even more than scraebins.

The cat scrambles up the post and stops at the door. I hop off its back and lose my balance because my whole body is trembling like a squirrel caught in a snowstorm. I catch myself on the wall and look back at the cat.

"Thank you," I whisper.

For a few moments, the cat looks at me with its bright amethyst eyes.

"Go on! Get out of here!" screams Mrs. Mildred Erdos. I look out across the yard. She's standing between the birdhouse and her porch waving a broom.

The cat jumps down and scurries toward the bank of the stream.

When I look away, I see Danni standing in her yard with her hands over her mouth.

"And don't you come over here, either, young lady," Mrs. Mildred Erdos shouts at Danni with the broom swinging above her head. Then she turns and walks into the log cabin, slamming the door behind her.

The Robins are still and quiet like a mantis resting on an ivy leaf. Mrs. Robin's head is tucked under her wing.

"I'm so sorry we've frightened you both," I say. A plate of

berries sits in the middle of the room. "Supper looks delicious."

Acting as if being transported home by a cat is as normal as collecting seedpods on a spring morning, I sit down to eat. After a few minutes, my limbs stop trembling and the Robins finally begin to nibble on their berries.

Before bed, Mrs. Robin wraps her wings around me in a warm hug. Mr. Robin pats my head with his beak.

I sleep great. When the morning sun nudges me awake, I sit up.

SMACK!

My head bangs right into the thick, sticky end of a branch.

13

THE SAPPY LOG

After the daze wears off, I follow the branch up through the birdhouse, making my way around buds and splintered bark. The branch pushes through my observatory and out the top of the birdhouse. There's no way the Robins brought this branch home. Even if they worked together, it's too big for them to wedge through the attic and down two floors to my room.

It *had* to be Danni. She must've come over after supper. Stretching my head around the end of the branch, I search for her. Sometimes, on days she doesn't go to school, she's outside early. But not today.

My stomach rumbles, so I climb down for breakfast. My arms and legs are more periwinkle blue than amaranth. And I haven't felt so hungry or well in days. Danni deserves a great big thank you for finding such a perfect, fresh branch.

After breakfast, I make sure there aren't any humans or cats around and then fly to Danni's yard. I feel weightless floating over the grass, past the pin oak, and onto the stump. The stream's water is clear. I hop over to take a sip. My cupped hands scare the tadpoles swimming near the streambed. They scurry off in all directions.

Back on the stump, the decaying wood is soft between my toes. I squat and lean against a ridge of bark, and then tuck my hands behind my head. Along the tree branches, pale green dots push through pink buds. One puffy, white cloud drifts across the blue sky. If I squint my eyes, it looks like Mrs. Mildred Erdos. Maybe she's a forest witch that floats from place to place until she rains down on kids who just want to be friends. I laugh. Witches aren't any more real than fairies.

"What's so funny?" Danni asks. My head bolts up. She sits down on her rock.

My eyes move from Danni to the water and trees around us. Then her house and then Danni again. Did she see me fly? My heart pounds. My hands are wet with sweat. Then I realize she couldn't have seen me fly. If she had, she would've pointed and screamed, *"You can fly!"*

"Hi Danni," I finally say. Then I point to the sky. "That cloud looks like Mrs. Mildred Erdos, doesn't it?"

Danni looks up and giggles. I let out a sigh of relief. She didn't see me fly.

After watching the cloud, Danni agrees, "It does look kind of like her." Danni looks at me and then says, "My parents said she and her husband built the log cabin from trees that grew here. They used to own a lot of this land."

"She has a husband?" I blurt out. That would mean there are two humans living in that house.

"Not anymore. He died years ago. She sold most of the land. Something about taxes. My parents said she only kept the lot with the log cabin. At least, that's what the real estate lady told them when we bought our house."

The story about Mrs. Mildred Erdos makes me sad. We need to talk about something happy. "I couldn't wait for you to come out so I could thank you for what you did. I feel wonderful today."

Instead of saying, *"You're welcome,"* Danni cocks her head to one side. "What are you talking about? What did I do?" Her eyes have that squinty look.

"The big, sticky branch—the one you put in the birdhouse for me last night," I point to the branch poking out of my observatory. "It was fresh and sappy and perfect." Danni is still confused, so I go on. "Didn't you come back out after supper and put it in the birdhouse for me?"

Danni looks at the birdhouse and then at me, shaking her head. "I didn't do that."

It *had* to be her. Who else is there? "Well, it's too big for the Robins. They didn't do it," I say.

Danni stands up and stares at the birdhouse holding a hand above her eyes to block the sun. "It didn't fall into the birdhouse," she says. "Someone had to open the roof." She gets quiet. Then her eyes grow as big as the sun. "Mrs. Erdos! She must have done it."

Mrs. Mildred Erdos, the possible floating forest witch? I don't think so. "But why would she?"

"I don't know," Danni answers.

Miss Evelie Poeley would say that thinking through even the silliest of ideas is smart, especially since we don't have a lot of ideas. "She does like to help Mr. and Mrs. Robin," I offer. "She shoos away cats, and there's a bowl of seeds on her porch."

"Maybe she was giving them the branch for their nest?" Danni suggests. Her voice is high. Her eyebrows are squished close together. Then she squeaks as she sucks in air while covering her mouth. When she moves her hand away from her face, she asks, "You don't think she knows about you, do you?" What a silly idea. That can't be it. "How could she? And even if she did, how would she know I was feeling ill and that I needed fresh sap to feel better?"

"I don't know." Danni stares out at the stream. The wind whistles through the trees. The stream gurgles as water loops and curls past roots that stick out from the bank. "Do you think it was Gigesdi?" Danni finally asks.

Now *my* hand flies up to *my* mouth. Is there another human I need to know about? I swallow a gulp of air and ask, "Who is Gigesdi?"

"The gray kitten. I saw her take you home last night," Danni announces.

That's right! Danni saw the whole thing. I remember Mrs. Mildred Erdos yelled at her after chasing away the cat. "But, how do you know the cat's name?" I ask.

"I named her. My parents said I could keep feeding her, and if she stays, we can keep her. But only as an outdoor cat."

My fingers curl. "Keep her? As a pet? But you just can't!" I can't tell if I'm angry, confused, or sad. My neck is hot, and my eyes sting.

"No, no, Zahra." Danni turns to face me. She looks scared. "I only meant that she could stay here and be our friend. I told you, she'd stay outside. I'd just make sure she had enough food. She could leave anytime. I want to help her because she's alone. Like you."

My fingers relax. I didn't think about it like that. There aren't any other cats around. It *is* possible Gigesdi lost her family, too. "I guess that would be okay." I don't want to argue. What she's doing is not really different from how Astrael and

I leave leftover nuts out for squirrels that live in nests above our colony. Well, I mean, *lived* in nests. They lost their homes, too. I push the thought away. "Why did you pick Gigesdi as her name?"

"It means purple in Cherokee. Since she has purple eyes like you, I named her in your honor."

Another odd word. "What's Cherokee?" I ask.

"Cherokee is the name of a group of people. I wrote a paper about the Cherokee Nation for school. They live not too far west of here."

Danni isn't making any sense, but I nod anyway. Someday I'll ask Miss Evelie Poeley or my parents about the Cherokee humans. "Gigesdi," I say. It's a good enough name. "Well, I don't think Gigesdi could cut a branch that big or drag it up to the roof of the birdhouse."

"Well, then I guess we're back to Mrs. Erdos," Danni declares. Then she pulls out her pencil and a notepad. "Now we just need to figure out why."

14

PEANUT BUTTER COOKIES

"She doesn't want me playing in her yard," Danni notes. She taps her pencil on the paper. "Maybe if I had a plate of my mother's peanut butter cookies, she wouldn't mind a visit."

Cookies are a sweet food that humans eat when they drink milk from a cow. Miss Evelie Poeley told us cookies take a long time to make. They don't grow in the forest. You have to grind wheat, collect eggs from birds, and boil the juice from a special kind of grass to make sweet crystals. After you mix everything together, you have to bake it in a hot oven, which is very dangerous.

I nod. I guess a treat might help if Danni and her mother want to do all that dangerous work. "What will you say when you get there with the cookies?"

Danni taps her pencil again. Then she says, "I'll ask if she needs help getting that branch out of the birdhouse. Then I'll start talking about ways it could've ended up there. Maybe that will get her to tell me what happened."

"I'll follow along and listen," I say. Danni's face wrinkles, so

I add, "I'll hide."

"If you're going to listen, I'll get her to sit outside with me. That way, you won't have to sneak into her house." Danni looks at Mrs. Mildred Erdos' back porch. Then she scribbles more swirly and straight lines on the notepad. "There's plenty of cover there. You need to check it out early and plan where to hide," she says.

I throw my hands into the air and yell, "You're brilliant, Danni!" She smiles so big her dimples dent her cheeks.

That afternoon, I sneak around to find a place to hide on Mrs. Mildred Erdos' back porch. There's a watering can against the house. The tree limbs of a Japanese maple that droop over the deck could work, too. But the best spot—the one where I know I'll be able to hear and see everything without being seen—is the large orange planter filled with four kinds of plants that grow tall and hang over the side.

Not long after I find a spot to sit in the planter, Danni arrives holding a plate. There's a strong nutty, sweet smell. It must be the cookies.

Danni moves the plate from one hand to the other. Her body sways back and forth. Finally, she taps on the door. Nothing happens. She wipes her hand on her pants, and then raises it again. But the door opens before she knocks. She jerks back and nearly drops the plate.

"Didn't I tell you to stay out of my yard?" Mrs. Mildred Erdos barks. Then she looks up. "Kids. They never listen, do they, dear?"

"Oh, uhm, hello, Mrs. Erdos," Danni stutters.

"Danishia, is it?"

"Yes, ma'am."

"Well, what are you doing here?"

Tell her about the cookies. Danni, in your hand—the cookies!
"What have you got there?" Mrs. Mildred Erdos asks, pointing to the plate that's shaking in Danni's grip.

"I, uhm, I brought cookies. I thought we could have a snack," Danni says.

"I guess she's going to try to worm her way over here with sweets, huh Herbert?" Mrs. Mildred Erdos says to the treetops. "Well, come inside, then." She opens the door wide.

Danni doesn't move. I'm holding my breath. Talk Danni! Say you want to sit on the porch. You can do this.

"Oh, well, I thought, uhm . . . it's such a pretty day. I thought maybe we could, I don't know—"

"Spit it out, young lady. You thought we could what?"

"I thought we could sit here. On your porch. It's such a pretty day."

"Very well. Pick a seat," Mrs. Mildred Erdos says. She points to two metal chairs and a table. Both had been painted long ago with pink, purple, and red roses. Rust is eating away at them. The paint is flaked. Most humans would've already turned them into tossasides.

Danni sits down and puts the cookies in the center of the table. Mrs. Mildred Erdos returns with cloth napkins and teacups.

"The tea will be ready in a few minutes. You do drink tea, don't you?"

"No, ma'am, not sweet tea. My parents don't let me have sugary drinks." Danni's voice is still shaky.

"But they let you have cookies? Humph. Well, I don't serve sweet tea in my fine china teacups. I'm steeping rosehip and hibiscus." Mrs. Mildred Erdos isn't getting nicer. Maybe she doesn't like peanut butter cookies.

"What's rosehip and hibiscus?" Danni asks.

"It's herbal tea. Don't worry. You'll like it fine. Now, what's this all about?"

"I just wanted to apologize for coming over here without permission. I didn't mean to upset you."

At least Danni isn't stuttering anymore. I step closer and move a leaf aside.

"I see. Well, no harm done. I just don't want you getting hurt. And while we're on the subject, you shouldn't be feeding that stray kitten. I don't want it hanging around here threatening . . ." Mrs. Mildred Erdos pauses and looks at the birdhouse. "My birds," she finally finishes. Then she straightens the cups and napkins.

Danni takes a breath and pushes up her spectacles. "Your birds are beautiful," Danni says. "I noticed a branch got stuck in the birdhouse." Danny points to the sappy stick. "It must've been windy last night. Can I help you remove it?"

That's it, Danni. Great job!

Mrs. Mildred Erdos looks at the birdhouse again. Then she looks at Danni. "No, no. I'll fix that another time. I'm sure the robins that live there can make use of it for their nests. And they can eat any bugs still crawling about." She takes a cookie and then looks at the sky again. "Remember when we had plenty of trees and no need for a birdhouse?"

Danni hangs her head. She needs to ask more questions. Where's her notepad? I step back and sit on a clump of dirt. Mrs. Mildred Erdos leaves to get the tea. When she returns, she asks, "Did you make these cookies?"

Danni looks up. "No ma'am, my mother made them."

"Well, please tell your mother she makes a delicious peanut butter cookie."

The two talk about the weather and Danni's school, except when Mrs. Mildred Erdos looks up to talk to Mr. Herbert Erdos. Soon the tea and cookies are gone. My arms are crossed. We're going to need a better plan.

"Thank you again, young lady. I'll wash and return the plate. Be careful walking back home. Poison ivy and snakes and such."

"Yes, ma'am," Danni says. Then she walks back to her house. Mrs. Mildred Erdos steps closer to the planter, so I duck behind a thick plant stalk, make myself as small as possible, and wrap myself in my wings. She lets the crumbs from her plate fall into the planter.

As soon as she's gone, I crawl over to the crumbs. One bite makes my jaw tight and my face tingly.

From the planter, I can see a window. It's open at the top. I look back at the birdhouse. Danni is nowhere in sight. She never found out if Mrs. Mildred Erdos put that branch in the birdhouse. Now it's up to me to get an answer. The Robins would not be happy with my idea, but staring at that open window I just know I have to take the chance.

15

THE GUEST

There's a box with flowers attached hanging off the window. Scrunched down behind yellow and orange marigolds, I peek in the window. I can see Mrs. Mildred Erdos' kitchen. She isn't there, so I crawl through the opening and stand behind a stack of dishes and bowls. On the counter, there's a line of tin cans, each a little taller than the last. That's where I decide to hide. Mrs. Mildred Erdos is talking in another room, but no one is talking back. For her, that's not unusual. "Perfect. I'll see you in a few minutes," she says.

CLACK!

She walks into the kitchen. My wings cocoon my body. After pushing my head out, I watch her pull cups and saucers out of a cabinet. It's difficult to see and stay hidden. I retract my wings and look for a better hiding place. In the corner, there's a large bowl of fruit. When Mrs. Mildred Erdos opens the door of the really big cabinet with the light, I run to the fruit bowl. From behind the oranges and bananas, I can see the whole kitchen.

Mrs. Mildred Erdos sets her yellow table with cups, saucers, plates, and forks. She puts out flowery napkins that match her marigolds. They also match the towel hanging on the oven door and the round mat in the center of the table.

DING! DONG!

What a horrible sound! It makes Mrs. Mildred Erdos leave the kitchen. I can hear her open a door.

My heart nearly bursts! What I feel is so strong. Scraebins? Then nothing. It's gone. My stomach tightens. It must be my imagination. I shake my head.

What I'm not imagining is a voice. There's someone talking. It's another human voice. When Mrs. Mildred Erdos walks back into the kitchen, she has a guest with her. The guest takes off a straw hat that has wildflowers poking out of a wide brim. She sits down. Her short hair is silver and yellow. It matches the flowers on her hat.

Mrs. Mildred Erdos places a teapot in the middle of the table. Then she puts cakes on a plate that she puts next to the teapot. She sits down with the straw-hat lady. The two talk—first about the weather, then about how to make the little cakes they're eating with their tea.

"Tell me about this little girl next door," the straw-hat lady says.

"She's not so little. She's eleven. She wanted to apologize for coming into my yard. I suppose the cookies were a peace offering," Mrs. Mildred Erdos reports.

"Well, that's not so bad. Why on Earth did you worry?"

Mrs. Mildred Erdos looks up at the ceiling. "Should I tell her, Herbert?"

"Tell me what?" the guest asks without looking up.

"Oh all right. My eyesight isn't all that good anymore, but when she talked about the stick, my suspicions were confirmed.

She knows about the scraebin in the birdhouse."

I fall backward and hit the wall behind me. My foot smacks an orange that rolls out of the bowl and across the counter.

THUD!

The orange hits the floor. I curl back into a ball tightly wrapped in my wings. I'm sure the two ladies can hear my heart thumping hard against my chest.

"What on Earth?" the straw-hat lady says.

"It's just an orange. I overfilled that fruit bowl." Mrs. Mildred Erdos picks up the orange and sets it on the table next to the cakes. Relief washes over me like a warm breeze. She doesn't know I knocked it loose.

But wait—she knows about me? She knows I live in the birdhouse?

"Ah. Well then, get back to your story. The girl knows about your young scraebin?"

Her young scraebin? I don't belong to Mrs. Mildred Erdos. My hands ball up before my wings retract. I don't belong to a human.

"It certainly explains why she's constantly looking at my birdhouse and prowling around my yard," Mrs. Mildred Erdos replies.

"I told you when you found the scraebin child that the birdhouse was a bad idea. You need to move her," the straw-hat lady says.

She put me in the birdhouse? But why? I fold my arms. That old lady human is *not* going to move me!

"No need to do anything rash. I'll simply keep the neighbor girl out of my yard," Mrs. Mildred Erdos says. She sips her tea. "Eventually, like all girls her age, she'll become distracted by music, movies, and other people her age. She'll forget all about my scraebin."

Danni needs to help me, not forget about me. I look at my feet and curl my toes.

"I don't know, Mildred. You know I've been against this whole idea since the day you found her. It's just not right."

Mrs. Mildred Erdos found me? I close my eyes hard and try to remember. She wasn't there. There were only the humans with loud machines, something big splashing in the stream, and then Mr. and Mrs. Robin.

"Clara, you worry too much. Herbert always said you were a worry-wart." The straw-hat lady is Clara—Mrs. Clara the Guest.

"The rules are in place for good reason. You don't go fooling with thousands of years of wisdom and tradition. The consequences could be devastating. You said yourself the girl next door knows about her." Mrs. Clara the Guest's voice is stern.

"When the Society was founded, people were kinder to Mother Earth," Mrs. Mildred Erdos says. Then she lets out a long sigh. "We didn't have pollution. There were no cities with skyscrapers and highways clouded with exhaust. Deforestation wasn't a word or even a notion." Mrs. Mildred Erdos stacks the dirty plates and clinks the silverware on top. "The world has changed so much in just the past 100 years, hasn't it, Herbert?"

"We're not meant to fix the world, Mildred. That was never our charge."

Mrs. Mildred Erdos stands up and slaps her cloth napkin on the table. Her long braid swings from side to side as she clears the dishes. "Thank you for coming, Clara. I'll see you on Tuesday at the meeting."

"You must know I have your best interests at heart," Mrs. Clara the Guest says as she stands. She folds her cloth napkin before putting it back down on the table.

Mrs. Mildred Erdos walks Mrs. Clara the Guest to the front door.

There it is again. Something, wait—no. It's gone. I miss my family so much.

Mrs. Mildred Erdos returns to the kitchen. The cups and saucers click and clack as she washes, dries, and puts them away. My head is bursting with questions. But I need to go back outside and meet up with Danni. I just have to wait for her to—

"You can come out now, dear," she says as she folds the damp dishtowel. Was she talking to Herbert again? "I know you're behind the fruit bowl."

Fruit bowl?

My neck turns hot, and my heart thumps. Mrs. Mildred Erdos is talking to *me*!

16

SCRAEBIN-SIZED

"Zahra, it's not polite to eavesdrop," Mrs. Mildred Erdos says.

She knows my name? But how? I stand up, but stay behind the fruit bowl. My feet feel like tree roots in soggy clay.

"I didn't think you'd remember the day I found you," she says. "She was still in shock, wasn't she Herbert? That was a treacherous day, indeed."

My stomach turns. I can barely catch my breath. Memories flash through my head. Floating on a stick in the stream. Hiding in the muddy bank. No food. Cold, hard dirt. Waking up in the birdhouse. Mr. and Mrs. Robin taking care of me. None of my memories include being rescued by a human. There are no pictures in my mind of an old lady human with a long white and gray braid wearing a green apron with lots of pockets.

"Come with me to the parlor and I'll tell you all about it, dear. I'm sure you have many questions." Unable to focus, I can't feel if it's safe to follow her. "I'm not going to hurt you. I've taken an oath to protect you. Come, now."

I clear my dry throat and then step out onto the counter right in front of Mrs. Mildred Erdos, an adult human. My body shivers. "An oath? What does that mean?"

"It means I made a promise to a secret society. A group of special humans who dedicate their lives to protecting scraebins. We're called the Society of the Sentinelia. I'm a Sentinelian. Have been for years, dear."

"I've never heard of a Sentinelian. Or a society of humans that helps us. Why haven't I heard this before?"

She closes her cabinet doors, crosses her arms, and leans on the counter. "How old are you, Zahra?"

"I'm eleven."

"She isn't meant to know about the Society just yet, Herbert. This will be difficult for her."

I look around to be sure there isn't another human lurking nearby. Mr. Herbert Erdos is supposed to be dead, but she keeps talking to him. "Where's the other person you keep talking to?" I ask.

Mrs. Mildred Erdos uncrosses her arms and moves her hands in and out of the pockets of her worn-out green apron. After a few minutes, she sits down and rests her hands on the table. "Oh dear, oh dear," she whispers as she shakes her head.

Her long twisted braid with feathers and leaves woven into it almost reaches the floor. It stands out against the dark, plain dress under her apron. "I didn't mean to upset you, Mrs. Mildred Erdos," I offer. Maybe she's just a sad, lonely widow. Harmless, I decide, unless a cat is climbing into her birdhouse.

She turns her head to look at me. "You know my name?"

"Yes. Danni told me. Is that okay?"

"Humph. Well, it's okay that you know my name," she says. She steps away. "Won't you come to the parlor and let me tell you about the day I brought you to the birdhouse?"

"And you'll tell me about the Society?" I ask.

"Yes, of course." She smiles as if she forgot she was upset. The window is still open. This is my chance to leave. I want to leave. But I need to know how I ended up in the Robins' birdhouse. I want to know about this Society. Most of all, I have to know if she knows what happened to my family.

In the parlor, the lemony, honey-sweet, fresh rain scent of magnolia blossoms fills the air. The entire wall at the front of the log cabin—including the door—is covered in petals, blossoms, buds, and leaves. All the petals are bright white, as if they were just picked today. It's odd, because it's too early for magnolia trees to bloom.

On another wall, there's a fireplace with wood stacked next to it. In the center of the room, there is a human-sized brown couch and two matching human-sized chairs. On the human-sized coffee table, there are scraebin-sized chairs and a couch. Scraebins sit on rocks or stacked twigs with seats made of leaves and petals. This furniture looks like human furniture, but smaller. I sit in the reddish-brown, high-backed chair with the blue cushion that faces Mrs. Mildred Erdos. She sits on her human-sized couch.

"I've had cookies and cakes today, and you've only had a bite or two. Can I get you a snack? Or some tea?"

"Do you have more of that red tea you gave Danni?" It smelled delicious.

"Rosehip and hibiscus. I most certainly do. That's a wonderful choice. I also have some acorn cakes you might like."

While Mrs. Mildred Erdos gets the tea and cakes, I look around. There are five lanterns, one in each corner of the room and one that hangs from the middle of the ceiling. Yellow light flickers from them.

"She'll love these, won't she, Herbert?" Mrs. Mildred Erdos says as she places a scraebin-sized plate with acorn cakes on the table next to me.

She places a scraebin-sized teacup and saucer next to the plate. Then she pours warm red tea out of a scraebin-sized teapot. Her fingers are so big she can't use the handle. Before sitting down, she gets her human-sized teacup and saucer from the kitchen.

After taking a sip, she asks, "Where would you like to start?"

I touch the plate with the acorn cakes. "Where did you get all of these scraebin-sized things? We don't have factories to make cups and saucers and teapots. We don't make human furniture."

Mrs. Mildred Erdos laughs. "You're right, dear. Scraebins don't make teapots or Queen Anne-style furniture. But humans do make them, even in small sizes."

"So, other humans *do* know about scraebins," I say.

"No, No. Not at all," she replies. "Humans make these for dollhouses. They're collectibles. People like to collect and display little houses filled with little furniture and household items, like teapots."

She's not making sense the way Danni doesn't make sense sometimes.

The chair's cushion is soft, and my tea cup is pretty, but using them is awkward. Too . . . human. But I can't let that distract me. I need more information. "Why don't you like Danni?" I ask.

Mrs. Mildred Erdos squints her eyes and scrunches her lips together. "I don't dislike Miss Danishia. Rather, I can't trust her. There's a difference."

"What's the difference?" I challenge, especially since I know Danni's trustworthy.

"Miss Danishia seems like a perfectly polite and nice young lady. I have no reason to dislike her. Honestly, she quite reminds me of my younger self. I, too, was passionate and inquisitive."

"Then why don't you trust her?" I ask.

"She's not a member of the Society of the Sentinelia. And humans who are not Sentinelia simply cannot be trusted in matters concerning scraebins."

17

THE SOCIETY

Sadness rolls over me like winter fog. Danni's my friend. She's going to help me find my parents. Maybe Mrs. Mildred Erdos doesn't trust her, but I do.

"You must take a bite of acorn cake and tell me what you think," Mrs. Mildred Erdos says. She leans in and pushes the plate closer to me with her wrinkled finger. I pick one up and take a bite. It tastes exactly like the ones Mother makes. My heart hurts. I miss her so much. "Well?" Mrs. Mildred Erdos asks.

"They taste just fine, thank you."

"Of course they do. It's a scraebin recipe." She sips her tea. "You're a little young to learn about Sentinelia, but circumstances call for an explanation. And I don't think there are any rules against telling a young scraebin. Although, if there are, I'm sure Clara will point them out at Tuesday's meeting."

I drop the acorn cake back on the plate. Mrs. Mildred Erdos raises her eyebrows.

"What does Sentinelia mean?" I ask.

"It comes from the word sentinel, which means to guard or

watch over. The Society of the Sentinelia is a group of humans who watch over and protect screabins."

"But why do humans need to protect us? We stay away from humans."

"We need to protect you from other humans, my dear. Thousands of years ago, screabins lived in harmony with humans. But as humans became more civilized and began building bigger and bigger communities, screabins started to disappear."

"Disappear? Like magic?"

"Not magic. How silly. Now pay attention," she replies. My face heats up, and I look down at my hands. Then she says, "Kidnapping."

My jaw drops open. "But why?"

"Screabins are small and nimble. They were captured and made to do various jobs to make humans' lives easier."

I feel like I can't breathe. "Were my parents and sister captured by humans?"

"No, no. Screabins haven't been kidnapped in centuries." She takes another sip. "Maybe she *is* too young for this, Herbert."

"I'm not too young," I say. "Please, tell me more."

"Well, considering what you've been through already, I suppose you earned the full explanation. Hasn't she, Herbert?" She looks up. Then she nods and continues, "A couple that lived on the edge of a town where many screabins had been put to work decided it wasn't right for humans to take screabins from their homes and separate them from their families. As a matter of fact, according to the Society Tomes, the couple talked about it so much, many of their family members and friends stopped talking to them."

"Society Tomes?" I ask.

"Yes, the Society Tomes. They are the books that contain the history, tradition, and rules of the Society," she answers. Then she goes back to her story. "That couple rescued many scraebins. A few close friends who believed as they did joined the effort. Then more people—more humans—were recruited. Together, they helped spread the word among scraebins that humans were not to be trusted. Among humans, they spread rumors that scraebins weren't real and those who believed in them weren't sane.

"They also made up stories about other little creatures that didn't exist, like elves. Many humans confused elves with scraebins." Mrs. Mildred Erdos' face lights up as if she were the one who came up with the plan to save and protect scraebins. "There were so many elf stories that the word scraebin died out among humans along with the memory of their existence."

What a tale. My eyes squint at Mrs. Mildred Erdos. "If humans don't know about us, why do you need to guard us?"

"She is a sassy little one, isn't she Herbert? It's scraebins like her that keep us in business."

How dare she call me sassy! "Excuse me?"

"My little Zahra, you are bold. And that boldness gave you the courage to reach out to Miss Danishia. Doing so put you and all other scraebins at risk."

I look down at the shiny table top. Danni isn't going to kidnap me. Or tell other humans about scraebins. It's time to change the subject. I look up and ask, "How did *you* become a Sentinelian?"

"Ah, well, where do I start?" she begins. "A Sentinelian has two jobs. One is to protect scraebins. The other is to seek out those who are worthy candidates for the Society so we always have plenty of Sentinelia to carry on the work."

"So, someone picked you?" I ask.

"Someone discovered me," she answers. She smiles. "Sentinelia are identified based on characteristics they possess. People who display all seven special characteristics are befriended. Then, after getting to know the candidate, there are tests the person must pass. When they pass the tests, they are brought to the local Society meeting for a final consultation. The local Society must then agree unanimously to accept the candidate as a Sentinelian. The process can take years."

"The meeting where you will see Mrs. Clara the Guest, is that the Society meeting?"

"Mrs. Clara Festmire?" Mrs. Mildred Erdos' smile gets so big her ears wiggle. "Yes, it is."

Mrs. Clara Festmire. Got it. "Could you please ask the Society of the Sentinelia if they've seen my family?"

Her smile disappears faster than a hummingbird's wings flutter. She has no words. She puts her hands in and out of the pockets on her apron. Then she gets up and clears the dishes. She comes back to the parlor and sits down.

"You wanted to know about the day I found you, didn't you? That's what we need to talk about next."

"Yes, but . . ." Has she already forgotten my question?

"I'd walked over to the stream behind the house. I don't often do that, you know. But I did that day. I had to shoo away that kitten. It appeared out of nowhere, and I didn't want it around my birdhouse. I should've known it'd come back. And now with Miss Danishia feeding it—"

"Was I with the cat?"

"Oh goodness no! You were wedged between a stick and a rock in the bank. And what a sad sight you were—all pink and droopy. I picked you up and asked your name. Without opening your eyes, you said 'Zahra.'" She looks away, but not up this time. Instead, she stares at the wall of magnolia blossoms. "Two robins had just taken refuge in my birdhouse. I remember they looked sad. That's why I placed you with them. I introduced you to the robins and asked them to take good care of you. Oh, I know they didn't understand the words. But they understood what I meant just the same. Then I took fresh twigs and placed them all around you."

"I remember!" I blurt out. "I remember all the twigs around me when I woke up."

"Of course you do, dear," she says. Then she pulls the clothes I was wearing the day I lost my family out of one of her pockets.

"Those are my clothes!" I cry out.

"Yes, dear."

I look down at my shirt and skirt. "Whose clothes am I wearing?"

"She's such a silly girl, isn't she, Herbert?" she replies to the ceiling. She looks at me and answers, "Those are your clothes. I gave them to you."

18

DANNI'S ROOM

"Pssst. Danni. Over here." I wave my hands from behind a clump of flowers in a planter. Danni is doing homework on the glass-topped table. If she'll just look this way, I can get her attention.

Gigesdi walks by the table. Danni looks away from her books, pulls something out of one ear, and then says hello to the cat.

"Gigesdi. Come here," I call out. If the cat walks this way, Danni might see me, too. The cat looks up. "Yes, that's it. Come here." I wave her over. Gigesdi ignores Danni and creeps to the planter.

"Zahra! What are you doing there?" Danni blurts out.

Finally! "Shhh!" I look around. "I didn't want Mrs. Mildred Erdos to see me," I say in a loud whisper. "I have so much to tell you. But not out here. Where can we go?"

Danni looks at Mrs. Mildred Erdos' house and then back at me. "She's not out right now, and her curtains are closed. She's not looking."

"She *might* be looking. Please, is there somewhere out-of-sight we can go?"

"Yes. Wait here," she says. She picks up her books and goes inside her house. When she gets back, she has a piece of salmon for Gigesdi and a box. Gigesdi rushes up to Danni, rubs her leg, and then takes the salmon.

Danni looks at me. "I'm going to put this box on the side of the planter away from her house. You hop in. Then I'll pop the lid on and carry you to my room," she says.

Jumping into a box sounds like a trap. Was Mrs. Mildred Erdos right about Danni? My eyes wander back to the log cabin.

"Look, there are holes in the sides and on top," Danni says. I look at the box. "You'll have light and air, but Mrs. Erdos won't be able to see you."

Danni puts the box down. Gigesdi rubs against it and purrs. The cat seems okay with the plan. But then, she's a cat. I roll my eyes and shake my head. I snuck into a human adult's house. This can't be worse.

I hop in.

"I'll be careful not to bounce the box," Danni assures me. Then she closes the lid.

After a deep breath, I feel better. The ride up to her room isn't too scary. Dots of light from the holes surround me. There's a soft blanket, too.

She puts down the box and takes off the lid. I jump out and land on a table. Wow! Her room. Is. Beautiful.

The walls are a light shade of blue. She has a lumpy blanket on her bed that looks like a pond with blue water, green grass, gray rocks, and a lily pad. There's an orange and yellow flower on the lily pad. Her furniture is painted to look like a forest—trees with brown and gray bark, leaves in different shades of green, and spindly vines. Between the trees are tall blades of grass and bright lavender, white, magenta, and yellow flowers.

The very best part of her room is the ceiling. It's dotted with white clouds. Some of the clouds are ... moving? "You can see the sky through your ceiling?" I ask as I stare at the clouds.

She looks up. "That's a skylight," she says. "On a clear night, I can lie on my bed and see the stars."

"Are all humans' bedrooms like this?" I look at Danni.

She shakes her head. "No."

"Why is yours?" If I were human, I'd *have* to have this bedroom.

"When my mom found out she had to move to North Carolina for her job—"

"North Carolina?" I didn't mean to interrupt, but Danni uses the strangest words.

"Yes, that's the state we live in, Zahra. Don't you learn about geography in school?"

"Sure. We learn how to get to neighboring colonies, the river—uhm, I mean stream—and where the bog is."

"Well, humans divide out land and give the pieces names. The piece we live on is called North Carolina."

"What piece of land did you live on before your mom had to move for her job?"

She looks away. "New York City. It's really far from here. And very different. The buildings stretch up to the clouds, and there are museums and the biggest library you could ever imagine," Danni says. She looks back at me. "But you might not like it there, because outside of Central Park, there aren't many trees."

It's hard to imagine humans needing houses that stretch up to the clouds, or living in a place without many trees. "What happened when your mom had to move? How did you get this room?" I ask.

"When my parents were only my foster parents—"

"Foster parents?" I interrupt again.

"Yes, my first mother was sick, and no one knew who my first father was. When I lived with my first mother, we slept wrapped in blankets next to the tall buildings. Outside." Danni's face has that droopy look again. No more interruptions. "A lady came and took me away. I don't remember much because I was only two years old. When they come and take you from your first mother, they bring you to foster parents. They let you live with them until your mom gets better or they find you a new mother."

Getting a new mother sounds awful. I don't want a new mother. I want *my* mother.

Danni's voice is quieter as she continues, "I lived with the cat foster parents—they had lots of smelly, scratchy cats—and then the rich foster parents with the nanny who read to me every night. When I was five, the lady with the clipboard took me to live with the Allmans. They're my parents now because they adopted me."

My mouth hangs open. What a story. Humans take children away from their parents and give them new families?

Wait! That's *exactly* what Mrs. Mildred Erdos did to me. The Robins are my foster parents.

Danni's still talking. I try to listen. "When they were my foster parents, they took me on long walks, and we had picnics in Central Park. We used to meet my new mother's parents there a lot. They are my grandparents. I miss them." Danni hangs her head. I stay quiet. "The park was my favorite place in the world. So, when we had to move here, my parents wanted to do something that would make me feel better. That's why they made me a Central Park bedroom."

"How wonderful," I say. But Danni doesn't smile.

"I guess," she says. "But I still miss New York City. And my grandparents." She looks up at me. "So, what did you come here to tell me?"

19

PLANT PLAN

D anni's done telling me about her family. Changing families and moving must be a hard story to tell. Talking about my own family isn't easy.

I stand up tall, then tell Danni everything about my visit with Mrs. Mildred Erdos. She listens without interrupting as I describe the Society of the Sentinelia and the day Mrs. Mildred Erdos found me.

"Gigesdi was there that day!" Danni blurts out as she leans in closer.

"I don't know of any other baby cats around here, so it must've been her," I agree.

"Gigesdi is looking out for you," Danni says. Her face isn't droopy anymore.

My eyes roll. "She's a cat. Cats attack scraebins."

"Most cats, yes," Danni agrees. "But Gigesdi was the reason you were saved from the stream after you lost your colony. Gigesdi got you home that day when you fell out of the tree. And today, if not for Gigesdi—"

"I know, I know. You wouldn't have seen me." It's all true.

But Gigesdi is a cat.

"I'm just saying *this* kitten, with eyes the *exact* same color as yours, is looking out for you," Danni says.

"I don't know. Maybe." The whole idea feels impossible. And even if Gigesdi is looking out for me, there isn't a scraebin alive who'd believe it.

"Let's get back to Mrs. Erdos. Do you think she might know where your family is?" Danni asks.

Now I feel like Danni looked when she was talking about her first mom and foster parents. "I don't think so."

"Well, maybe she can help us find them. If anyone can help, it's her. We should ask her. Now that you've had a nice visit with her, she'll listen to us," Danni chatters quickly. "Let's talk to her soon."

"There's something else you should know," I look into Danni's big green eyes. "Mrs. Mildred Erdos doesn't trust you. She said humans who aren't members of the Society can't be trusted. She told me to stay away from you."

Danni frowns and looks away. Then she turns back to me and asks, "Do you believe her?"

"No, Danni. Not at all. I trust you. I don't think you'd hurt me or any other scraebins. You're my friend." My heart is beating as fast as my words pop out.

"You're my friend, too."

That's a relief. "Thank you," I say. "I do think Mrs. Mildred Erdos might be able to help. If she got to know you like I know you, maybe she'd trust you." I don't completely believe that, but do hope so with all my heart.

"I suppose you're right," Danni agrees. "If she's a member of that Society, she must watch over other scraebins. Maybe the others have heard of your family.

"Exactly," I say. "We need to talk to the other scraebins she protects. We have to get Mrs. Mildred Erdos to introduce us to them."

Danni pushes up her spectacles. "But why did she put you in the birdhouse instead of with other scraebins?"

That same thought crossed my mind. "Maybe she doesn't watch over other scraebins. She's pretty old. And she's a widow."

"Well, we need to find out," Danni takes out a notebook and pencil.

"First, we need to get her to trust you," I say. "She likes peanut butter cookies and tea. I'll tell her I'd like to come over again for tea, and then we'll both show up. If you have cookies, she'll let you stay."

"That's not a bad idea," Danni agrees. "But I think I'll have to do more than bring cookies this time." Danni taps the pencil on her head. "A plant!" she says. The tapping stops.

"A plant?" I say, confused, but curious.

"Yes. I've got begonia stems rooting in a cup of water." Danni drops the pencil and notepad and walks over to the window. She takes the cup with leaves poking out and brings it back. "See!" She pulls the leaves out of the water. A twisted clump of pale white roots dangles from the stem. Water drips down and splashes back into the cup. "It's ready to be planted." She drops the stem and stands up. "I can plant it in the clay pot I made at school in my art class." She grabs the pot off a shelf. "I painted roses on it. They match the ones on the chairs on her porch."

"That's really pretty," I say. The flowers do look like the ones on the chairs. It's a perfect gift for Mrs. Mildred Erdos.

"Thank you. I'm sure my mom has potting soil in the garage."

Danni writes on her notepad.

"Can you plant it tonight?" I ask. The sooner we meet with Mrs. Mildred Erdos, the sooner we can find my family.

"Sure," Danni says as she writes.

"Great! Tomorrow morning while you're at school, I'll tell Mrs. Mildred Erdos that I want to visit for tea in the afternoon. I'll tell her I have more questions about the day she found me. Then, when you get home, we can go to her house. With cookies and a plant, she can't turn you away. Then she'll see for herself you're wonderful and trustworthy."

Danni pushes up her spectacles. "So, what do we do if she doesn't know any other scraebins? I just really think if she did, you'd be living with them."

At first, there's nothing much to say. Then I remember the guest. "She knows other Sentinelia. They meet at Tuesday. I don't know where Tuesday is, but that's what I heard her tell Mrs. Clara Festmire. She's a Sentinelian, too, I think. And if she's one, and there are others—"

"They might know scraebins who might know something about your family!" Danni finishes my thought.

"Exactly!" I say.

20

TEA & DANNI

"What is *she* doing here?" Mrs. Mildred Erdos says when she opens the door. She looks Danni up and down. "What's that you've got? A sickly plant?"

"I rooted my begonia and made this for you," Danni says without a shake in her voice this time. "And I've got peanut butter cookies in my backpack. May we please come in?"

"We? I had plans this afternoon with Zahra. I wasn't expecting anyone else. I'm not prepared." Mrs. Mildred Erdos blocks the door with her body the same way Mr. Robin did when I was grounded. "And you, little one. Riding her shoulder? Out in the open?" She shakes her head.

"Her parents are still working, and no other neighbors are out," I say. Checking for humans is all I do lately.

"But—" Mrs. Mildred Erdos tries to reply before Danni cuts her off.

"Zahra stayed on my left shoulder so my head and body blocked her from being seen by nosy neighbors peeking through the blinds from across the street." Danni shows her dimples with a wide grin.

Mrs. Mildred Erdos' shoulders sink with a sigh. "Scraebins were much easier to watch over when we were young, weren't they, Herbert?"

"I would very much like to be your friend, Mrs. Erdos," Danni says. She holds the plant up.

"And I would very much like my Sentinelian and my best friend to get to know each other," I add. "That's why I made tea plans with you."

"Humph," Mrs. Mildred Erdos grunts. Then she crosses her arms over her apron.

"I've never seen an apron with so many pockets," Danni observes. She's still holding the plant up. Her arms must be getting tired. "It's beautiful, Mrs. Erdos. Did you make it?"

"I did," Mrs. Mildred Erdos replies. Her arms stay folded.

"Twenty-one pockets. I bet that's handy. I'd love an apron with twenty-one pockets," Danni says.

"Did you make that planter?" Mrs. Mildred Erdos asks.

"I painted it, yes, ma'am. I thought you'd like it because it matches your patio furniture." Danni points to the roses.

"That is quite nice," Mrs. Mildred Erdos agrees as she unfolds her arms. She takes the plant from Danni. Then she looks at me. "I suppose you told her all about the Sentinelia?"

"Yes," I answer.

She looks at Danni again. "You say you have peanut butter cookies in that backpack?"

"Yes, ma'am. And I also brought snickerdoodles."

"Is that so? Well, come in then. I suppose I could make a larger pot of tea."

We all go to the living room. The scraebin-sized furniture on the coffee table immediately grabs Danni's attention.

"It's like a little scraebin living room on top of your coffee table. It's so welcoming. Is it dollhouse furniture?"

"That's very astute, Miss Danishia," Mrs. Mildred Erdos answers. Then she reaches into one of her pockets and pulls out a pillow. "My Herbert made this for a family we used to watch over. There were seven more just like it." She holds the pillow out for Danni.

"It's beautiful, but I'd rather not touch it. I wouldn't want anything to happen to it."

"Oh, go on. You can't hurt it. My Herbert put many hours of work and great care into everything he crafted. What he made was meant to last for generations."

Danni carefully takes the pillow and holds it up to her eyes. Then she hands it to me. It's as silky as Mother's hair. And it's more colorful than a sunset after a thunderstorm.

"What happened to the family you used to watch over?" I ask.

"They moved on when the house next door was built," Mrs. Mildred Erdos answers. Then she squints at Danni. "Miss Danishia's house. They lived in the pin oak tree. In the large knothole about midway up the trunk."

"Does someone else look after them now?" Danni asks.

I wonder the same thing.

"I don't know." Mrs. Mildred Erdos whispers as she turns away.

We need information that will lead us to my family, so I ask, "Who do you look after, now?"

"You mean besides you, dear?" Mrs. Mildred Erdos replies. "You're quite enough. A sassy, bold little being, quite like one of the very first scraebins I ever met."

Unbelievable! She called me sassy *again*!

"Remember her, Herbert? Little Twinka. Her parents had a

time keeping her out of trouble."

She's off track already. "Mrs. Mildred Erdos, I know you don't trust Danni, but I do. And she's going to help me find my parents. And we were hoping—"

"See Herbert? Trouble," she says to the ceiling, cutting me off.

Ignoring the ceiling, Danni asks, "Do you know where we might be able to find them? Have any of the other Sentinelia talked about Zahra's family?" Danni's completely over the nervousness she had around our neighbor.

Mrs. Mildred Erdos dips a snickerdoodle in her tea. The warm red liquid bleeds into the light brown cookie. "You're from New York City, aren't you, Miss Danishia?" she finally says after eating the cookie.

"Yes, ma'am."

"Lots of big buildings. Not many trees."

"Yes, ma'am."

"There are no screabins in New York City. Not anymore. And there aren't many around these parts any longer, either." Mrs. Mildred Erdos dips another cookie.

"So, you haven't heard anything about her parents?" Danni's on a roll. If anyone can get Mrs. Mildred Erdos to help us, it's her.

"Most of the screabins left when all these houses were built. A few remained. They lived in the woods on the other side of the stream. But now," Mrs. Mildred Erdos pauses to take another bite. "Now, they're building over there, too. People are taking more and more land. They're knocking down more and more trees. I don't know where the screabins here will go next."

"That's just awful." Danni puts down her tea. It clinks

when it hits the saucer. There's a long stretch of quiet. When everyone's done snacking, Danni places the leftover cookies in a jar on Mrs. Mildred Erdos' counter. Then she washes the teacups, saucers, and teapot.

"You're quite the polite little helper, aren't you?" Mrs. Mildred Erdos points out.

"Thank you for a nice afternoon. I should get Zahra back before my parents get home."

"Get her back?" Mrs. Mildred Erdos stops and then points to me. "She can fly back on her own."

Oh no! Why did she tell her?

Danni's eyes grow bigger than a full moon. "You *can* fly! I knew it. So you have wings?"

"Of course, she has wings. She's a scraebin," Mrs. Mildred Erdos says. Her eyes are slits, like the moon when it's mostly in shadow. "You certainly have a lot to learn about your friend."

"Why didn't you tell me, Zahra? This is amazing!" Danni says. I feel bad for not being honest. "Please, will you show me, Zahra?"

This was not how I imagined telling Danni I can fly. After letting out a gruff sigh, I say, "If you promise not to call me a fairy, I'll show you. But you won't be able to see my wings. And once I begin flying, you probably won't be able to see me."

"Are your wings invisible? Do they make you invisible? Are they magic? How does it work?" Danni rattles off without giving me a chance to answer.

"Her wings are simply a color we can't see," Mrs. Mildred Erdos explains. "When she extends them, the wings cover her body to protect her from predators. And humans." She turns to me. "No, go on. Get back to the birdhouse before the Allmans return home from work. Shoo!" She waves her hand.

"Bye, Danni," I say.

Flying home, I hear Danni squeal and say she can hardly believe what she's seeing. And not seeing. Then she runs home. From her yard, she turns and looks at the birdhouse. I'm standing in the doorway. I nod and wave. She waves back and then disappears inside.

I'm sure Mrs. Mildred Erdos sees she can trust Danni. I'm excited, too, because now we have a clue. It's something I just know will lead us to my family.

21

THE CLUE

Snickerdoodles are my new favorite food. The nutty, cinnamon flavor dances on my tongue like the petals of a daffodil in the spring wind. The sweet tingle in my jaw is as wonderful as the rainbow spray from a waterfall hitting me in the face.

"What clue did she give us?" Danni asks.

She's sitting cross-legged on a round jade-green pillow on the floor of her bedroom. Her hair is pulled into two ponytails that start at the top of either side of her head. I'm facing her from the hard, blue couch in the living room of a dollhouse Danni pulled from a box in her basement. My hair is the same as always—straight and gray. I wonder what I'd look like with ponytails of curly, dark hair tumbling down the back of my neck.

"Well?" she persists.

Oh, right. The clue. "Construction," I say. I take another tingly bite.

"Construction?" Danni doesn't catch on to this important detail.

"Yes. The loud noise, the big humans, and the machines I remember from that day—those humans must be building a human house where my colony's tree stood."

Danni stands up and runs to her window. "Of course! If we go to the construction site across the stream, we'll find more clues that can lead us to your family!"

I put my feet on the orange footstool and pick up another piece of snickerdoodle. "When can we go?"

"First, we have to scope out the area." Danni moves from the window back to her pillow. She grabs a notepad and pencil on the way. Her drawers and closets must be filled with pencils and notepads. "Then, we need to figure out which lot they were bulldozing the day you got lost. How long ago was that, exactly?"

She taps the top of the pencil on the notepad. I slide back in my seat, sit straighter, and plop my feet on the floor. "Two full moons ago. I remember, because I waited until the full moon before getting up early to collect the moss."

Danni looks at me the way Miss Evelie Poeley did when she wasn't happy with my answer. "And what day was that, exactly?" she asks with a breath between each word, as if I didn't understand the question.

It's frustrating that *she* doesn't understand my answer. Maybe she's distracted by imagining what it'd be like to have long, straight gray hair like mine. "I just told you. It was two full moons ago."

"But what was the date?" she persists.

I shake my head. "I don't know. We don't—"

"Never mind," she interrupts and looks away. "We can figure it out." Danni pulls out her phone and begins tapping. "I'll just look up the date of the full moon in February."

After another bite of the delicious snickerdoodles, I have a question. "How will we find out which place was bulldozed that day?"

"We'll ask one of the construction workers," she answers, still tapping and swiping her phone screen. "February fourteenth." She scribbles on her notepad.

I stop mid-chew. Our plan absolutely *cannot* involve me talking to any more adult humans. "I think you need to be the one to ask."

Danni looks at me and pushes her spectacles up her nose. "Yes, I suppose you're right. You'll have to hide in my backpack."

Hide? In a backpack? "That doesn't sound comfortable. Or safe." The box wasn't horrible, but that was a short trip to her bedroom. A backpack ride to a place far away sounds scary.

"I'll put a box inside. And some newspaper and cotton to make it comfortable."

How did she know what I was thinking? I just stare, unable to say anything. Even with newspaper and cotton, this part of the plan isn't Danni's best idea.

"And a few pieces of my mom's snickerdoodles," she adds.

"That just might work," I agree. How bad can it be if there are snickerdoodles?

"And." Danni begins drawing on her notepad. "I can run a metal straw from the box out through the zipper on the side. That way, you'll be able to hear everything. I'll tape it to keep it in place."

"That sounds good." Now she's making sense. "I want to hear everything those construction worker humans say."

"We have a teacher workday tomorrow," Danni says. She's still marking up her paper. "That means no school. It's the perfect time to go. It's during the week, so the construction workers should be there. Let me check the weather." She goes back to her phone.

"It's going to be a warm, sunny day," I report.

Danni looks up, "How do you know that?"

"Know what?" I ask.

"Tomorrow's weather?"

"My feet." I point my left foot at Danni. "See?"

Danni puts down the phone, notepad, and pencil and moves closer. "What am I supposed to see?"

I turn my foot and look. "I don't know, exactly. But my feet can tell what the weather's going to be. I guess they tell my brain."

"You can sense the weather through your feet?" Danni's eyebrows rise up high. She studies my feet with her eyes. She pokes my toe with her pencil.

"Hey!" I yelp.

She backs away. "Sorry. I was just curious. I'm so sorry."

"It's okay," I say. Then I explain. "My sister Astrael told me our feet pick up clues from the air and ground and trees. They send the information through our bodies to our brains. Then we know."

"That's . . . the coolest . . . thing . . . I've EVER . . . heard!" Danni exclaims as she cocks her head, still staring at my toes.

"Maybe you could do the same thing if you didn't wear shoes," I offer.

"I wish!" Danni grabs her phone. "Let me see if your prediction matches my weather app." She taps and waits. Then she shakes her head. "No, according to my app, there's a sixty-eight percent chance of rain. Anything over forty percent, and my mom sends me out with an umbrella."

Danni and her human talk! I roll my eyes. "Well, my feet

don't lie. It's not going to rain."

Danni looks at both of my feet again, which are now crossed on the orange footstool. She puts her pencil down and looks at me.

"Yes, but we need a Plan B in case it rains," she says.

"That's silly. It's not going to rain." I grab the last crumb of snickerdoodle. My feet certainly know better than a flashy piece of metal and glass.

"Well, just in case. You never know." She picks up her pencil and taps her head.

Swallowing hard, I counter, "I *do* know. It's really *not* going to rain." My feet hit the floor of the dollhouse, and I stand up tall.

"Okay, but if it does, we'll just explore the lot that has the most construction over the weekend. My app says Saturday will be sunny and dry."

"Will construction worker humans be there on Saturday?" I bark.

She looks up. "Probably not."

"Then who will we ask to find out which place they bulldozed two full moons ago?" I really like Danni, but she can be difficult.

"I suppose we could find a nearby house with people living in it and ask them." Danni scribbles on her notepad again.

It's not going to rain, so there's no need for this Plan B talk. The weather is never a surprise, because my feet work just fine. Instead, we need to focus on finding more clues tomorrow. It's possible we might even find my family. Mother is probably making dandelion broth right now, with violet petals and grass seedpods. I can almost smell it.

"Are you okay?" Danni asks.

"Yes, why?"

"A tear just slid down your cheek."

I wipe my sleeve across my face. "I'm fine. I was just thinking about my mother's dandelion broth."

"Oh Zahra, we're going to find them. I promise."

"I know," I say. "I should go. I want to take a nap in the knothole before I go home."

"That's a good idea. I'll meet you tomorrow after my parents leave for work. When you hear their cars leave, be ready to fly over. I'll be waiting in my driveway with my bike." Danni shows me the map of her house and our yards that she drew on her notepad. She points to where she'll be waiting. "And if looks like it's going to rain—"

"It's not! Just trust me."

Danni puts her notepad and pencil down next to her phone. "Okay, Zahra. I'll see you in the morning."

22

THE CLOAK

"Not a cloud in the sky," I say as I land on Danni's shoulder. "My feet never lie."

"Okay, okay. Wait until you see what I did to my backpack," Danni says as she puts it in the basket of her bike. I can already smell snickerdoodles.

Inside is a box with holes in the lid. Rolled yellow fabric with green leaves sewn in a pattern sits against the walls. The bottom is covered with stuff she calls cotton balls and crumpled newspaper. She put the snickerdoodle pieces inside a bottle cap—which looks like a tossaside to me—in the corner. Two tubes stand straight up and poke outside the box. "Why *two* tubes?" I ask.

She moves the snickerdoodles to a different corner and puts more cotton around the tubes. "While I was working on this last night, I thought you needed some light. I didn't want you to be in a dark box in my zipped up backpack."

She doesn't know scraebins can see in the dark—even on the darkest, moonless nights. I should tell her, but she went to all this trouble. I don't want to hurt her feelings. "That was thoughtful. Does one of the tubes make light?" I ask.

"What? No," Danni replies. "See that plastic stick near the side?" She picks it up. The stick is as long as I am tall. A bubble moves in the yellow liquid inside when she moves it.

"Yes, What's that?"

"It's a glow stick. I'm going to crack it to make it shine light right before we leave."

"Really?" That sounds like magic, but, of course, it can't be.

"Yes. The tube is filled with chemicals that make it glow. I just have to break the seal to make them mix together."

Maybe the chemicals are magic? Like a potion? It's hard to follow what Danni says. Meanwhile, she hasn't answered my question. "But what about the second tube?" I ask again.

She looks up at me with pursed lips. "Right. I'm getting to that. When I put the glow stick inside, I thought it would be even better if you could see *outside*. So I made a periscope. It has tiny mirrors in it. The mirrors are at an angle. Climb inside and look right here," she points to an opening in the tube.

After a deep breath, I climb inside the box. This is still scary, especially with the magic potion chemicals light stick thing I don't need. I step up to the tube and look through the hole. I see Danni's bicycle, the house behind her, and her arm. I look up, "This is great! You're so smart."

"Not really. I just looked it up on the internet," she says with a hand on her hip.

"Well, you have a very smart internet."

Danni giggles. She gives the cotton balls one last nudge. "Are you ready?"

"Yes." My stomach flips and flops when I think about finding my family. Or maybe my stomach isn't ready to ride on Danni's bicycle in a cotton-filled box with a chemical stick that glows. "Thank you for doing all this, Danni."

"One more thing. This other tube will help you hear, but you can also whistle into it to get my attention if something goes wrong. Can you whistle?" I step to the end of the other tube and whistle. Danni's jaw drops. "Wow! That was beautiful," she says. "You sound angelic when you do that."

"Angelic?" She uses so many odd words.

"Yes, like angels from Heaven."

"I don't know what angels or Heaven are, but Mother says I sound like wind blowing through a glade on a winter's day."

Danni raises an eyebrow, "Same thing, I suppose."

She grabs the yellow stick and snaps it. It *does* glow. She places it in a piece of the crinkled newspaper. The light makes the cotton glow. A stack of two cotton balls in another piece of newspaper makes a comfortable seat. I drag the cap closer so I can snack. Then I lean closer to the periscope tube and watch.

We ride and ride. It's a little bumpy, but the cotton and newspaper makes it comfortable.

Then, out of nowhere, I smell it! I drop the cookie and whistle for Danni.

She stops.

I tumble forward. Snickerdoodle pieces fly up and bounce off the box top and sides. I land on the roll of fabric. My feet are tangled in crumpled newspaper.

"Are you okay? What's wrong?" Danni cries out. She unzips her backpack and flips the lid off the box.

"That smell. It's her, I just know it is!" I yell back.

Danni puts her finger next to me so I can lean on her and pick newspaper out of my toes.

"Who? Who do you smell?"

Sadness, joy, hope, and fear swirl through me like dry leaves and dirt before a storm. I scramble to the top of the backpack and look around. We're near the construction. The dry, hard stench of nails and wood dust is strong. But I can also smell Astrael. Well, not her, but her cloak. The one Aunt Lily Aylward made out of goose feathers and lavender stalks soaked in acorn oil. She wore it every evening during the cool seasons.

"My sister's cloak. It's nearby." I look all around, but I'm confused from riding in the box. Did we cross the stream? We must have.

"What does it look like? I'll help you," Danni offers with an outstretched hand.

Standing still, ignoring her hand, I draw in a long breath. Then I fly.

"Zahra!" Danni gasps. "I need to follow you. I can't see you. Please be careful!" She sounds scared. I retract my pectoral wings so she can see my body, then slowly drift with the wind, following the scent until—

THUMP!

"Zahra!" Danni screams.

I land in her hands. They're shaking. Next to us is the tall blue plastic box that stopped me. I crawl to the edge of Danni's hand, searching for what I know is here. Somewhere.

"Zahra, I need to put you back in my backpack," she begs. "There are construction workers on the other side of this port-a-john. They'll see you."

"There it is!" I point to the ground at the corner of the plastic box.

Danni puts me down, and we both dig around the cloak. Then we slide it out of the sand and dirt. Danni holds it up to her eyes. She lifts the sleeves, opens it, turns it, and then finally hands it to me. "It doesn't look like she was in it," Danni says. "There's no sign of her."

I pull the cloak to my face and hug it as if it were Astrael. Maybe holding it will somehow lead me to her.

"Can I please put you back in the backpack?" Danni asks. "I really need you to hide, Zahra. Please."

I nod. She's right. Inside the box, I wrap myself in Astrael's cloak and listen through the other tube. The banging and whining of human tools grows horribly loud. We're close to the construction worker humans. I sink deeper into the cloak. And the cotton.

"Excuse me, sir," Danni says to one of them. "Can you tell me which lot was cleared on February fourteenth?"

He laughs and then calls out, "This little girl wants to know which lot was cleared on Valentine's Day."

Another yells back, "Well, isn't that romantic? I suppose it'd be that one."

"He says it was that one—that two-story with the wrap-around porch," the voice close to us says. "Why do you ask, young lady?"

"Thank you, sir. I was just curious. Have a nice day." Danni climbs on the bicycle, and we start moving again.

"You, too," the construction worker human says.

We don't ride long before we stop again. "There are too many people walking around for you to come out," Danni reports in a loud whisper. "Look through the periscope. The house doesn't have walls yet."

I look and immediately see the house and, just beyond it, the stream. Sadness crawls down my spine. My hands shake. On the other side of the stream that I can clearly see through

Danni's periscope tube is the old cedar tree that we could see from the pecan tree where my family lived—the pecan tree that's now completely gone. Like it never existed. No stump. No pieces of drying bark. No arch of fallen branches with dead leaves. Nothing.

I drop down on the cotton floor of the box and cry.

"Let's go home, Zahra," Danni says.

When we stop in her driveway, I'm finished crying and ready to go back to the Robins' house. Danni opens the backpack. Holding my sister's cloak close to my chest and without saying a word, I fly away.

23

NIGHT FLUTTER

C urled up in bed in my sister's cloak, I think about that skeleton of a human house at the construction site. It was two stories tall, just like Danni's. Probably only one human family will live there. Humans tear down trees that are homes to colonies of scraebins, squirrels, birds, and insects to build houses filled with human-made things. Things that will one day become tossasides.

Mrs. Mildred Erdos' house is much smaller than the house at the construction site. There are trees and rocks all around her log cabin. Where there's grass that crept over from other people's yards, it's tall and seedy. But even she has more rooms and furniture than one human needs. Danni and her family are living in the house that stands next to a tree where another scraebin colony used to live. Danni is my best friend, but is she different from other humans?

I breathe in the smell from Astrael's cloak. My hands finally stop shaking.

It looked like the cloak was dropped. Maybe it fell as she flew away to escape the machines and humans.

Holding the cloak even tighter, I try to feel them. I picture my family flying away. Looking for me. Finding shelter. My sister, parents, and the others from our colony must be alive somewhere. But where?

I imagine Mother, Father, and Astrael living in a nearby knothole. Then I think about finding them, running into Mother's arms, hugging Father and Astrael, and then all of us crying and laughing together.

But I know they're not nearby. If they were, I'd feel them.

There must be more clues at the construction site. I have to go back. At night, when the humans aren't there. That means Danni can't be there, either, which is a problem. Danni knows the way. I was in a box in her backpack, where I watched pieces of trees and houses swoosh by through a tube.

Eyes closed, I focus on the memory of the ride. We passed Mrs. Mildred Erdos' house, so that's the direction I need to travel. The new houses are being built across the stream. The bike moved as fast as I can fly, and it didn't take long to get there, so it's not too far.

My eyes fly open. I can do it!

When the Robins are asleep, I leave, but not out the front door. I don't want to wake them. Instead, I go through the roof in my observatory, careful to make as little noise as possible when I close the shingle. The skies are clear. Moonlight bounces off the water in the stream, wet leaves, and white rocks along the bank. Before landing on the pin oak, my wings are already tired. I'm tired. A rest in the large knothole helps.

As the sap makes me stronger, I come up with a new plan. I decide to climb across a branch that reaches a branch from a tree on the other side of the stream. A walk along the bank, against the current, will lead to where Danni took me. To save energy, my plan is to fly only if there's danger.

My plan works. And I did it without a pencil or notepad! I stay close to the bank and walk faster and faster. The smell of wood dust and nails hits my face. I'm close. My heart pounds when I see the blue plastic box. I walk to it.

"Oh! No, no, no!" I blurt out. I'm stuck!

A spider's web tangled my feet. A web I should've seen. I try to kick my feet free. I pull at the web. But the harder I kick and pull, the tighter the web holds me. Now the sticky strands are keeping me from extending my wings, too.

I stop moving, hang my head, and sob.

Why did I come out here on my own? What if I can't free myself? Will a hawk eat me? Or will the construction worker humans find me in the morning?

"YAH!" I holler. A wet, scratchy tongue slides up the back of my arm.

It's Gigesdi! Her gray fur looks silver in the moonlight, and her amethyst eyes glow. She licks away the sticky strands of web. Then she tucks her front paws under her belly. She wants me to get on her back. I climb up and bury my hands and face in her fur. Part of me wants to stay and find more clues. But a bigger part is happy when Gigesdi turns away from the construction site and scampers back in the direction of the birdhouse.

She climbs a tree and crosses the stream using a branch as a bridge to the pin oak—just like I did. But instead of climbing down and walking me to the birdhouse, she steps into the large knothole and curls up into a fluffy ball. She's soft and warm.

If my family saw me cuddled next to her, they'd be horrified. Cats are supposed to be dangerous. But this one isn't dangerous at all. Danni was right. Gigesdi looks out for me like the

Robins. She protects me.

Breathing in and out with this silvery, gray baby cat, my heart tells me not all cats are dangerous. Maybe we need to learn about a cat before we decide if it's good or bad.

Then I think about Danni. She's young, like me. She didn't build her house. Someone else did. She lives there because that's where her parents said she has to live. She didn't even know scraebins existed until she saw me and splashed into the stream.

Most humans don't know about scraebins. They don't know that when they kill trees to build houses, they're tearing down our homes. But they do know they're killing trees.

I let out a long sigh. Humans confuse me more than anything Miss Evelie Poeley taught us.

Gigesdi wraps her tail around me and purrs.

A night in the knothole with Gigesdi made me feel strong and healthy. I leave before the sun is up and climb back through the roof of the birdhouse. The Robins never knew I was gone. After eating a few seeds, I fly to Danni's window and tap. She's in bed, awake, reading a book.

Another tap.

She sees me, drops her book, and runs to the window. "What are you doing here?" she asks as she pushes open the window.

24

SAVE THE TREES

"We really need to talk," I tell Danni as I step into her hand.

"You're upset with me, aren't you? And with all humans. I know *I'd* be if I were a scraebin," she says as she walks across her room.

In the dollhouse, I sit on the hard blue couch. "I wanted to be upset with you," I say. She goes back to the window to close it. "I think I was when we got back yesterday."

"I thought so," she says without looking at me. "You didn't say anything. You just left." Danni plops down on the pillow that looks like a lily pad.

"I know. I'm sorry." It was rude to leave like that, especially after she did so much work to help me.

"It's okay. I understand," she says. "I did some research after you left. There are groups of people who work to protect trees. And even plant new ones." She's pulling on the ends of her hair. No braids or ponytails this morning.

"So, some humans do think it's terrible to kill trees?" I ask. I sure hope it's true.

"Of course!" she finally looks up at me. "My grandparents in New York love trees and would never hurt them. They're part of a group that plants saplings all over the place. And we used to have picnics under the trees in Central Park."

"There are a lot of humans who think it's okay to kill trees, especially if they're building houses like, well . . . yours." That was mean. And I'm not even mad anymore.

Danni hangs her head. "I know."

"I'm glad your grandparents love trees," I say to try to make her feel better.

"I love them too, Zahra." She lifts her chin, pushes up her spectacles, and looks straight into my eyes. "I really do. And after seeing the construction site, I want to do something to change things."

"Change things? What would you change? And how? You're just a child."

"So are you. But we're smart, aren't we?"

What she says is true. But that doesn't mean we can make a difference. Her eyes shift back and forth between me and, I don't know, the walls, I guess.

"Think about it, Zahra. What would be the point of helping you find your family if the same thing is just going happen to you and other scraebins all over again?"

"You've really thought a lot about this. What do you plan to do?" Danni's like Gigesdi—a protector. Kind-hearted and generous. I'm sure she really does have a plan.

"I'm going to start an Arbor Club at school. If other students feel the same, maybe we can plant trees in the new neighborhood where they cut them all down."

That's a good idea, but after seeing the construction site, I want more. "Wouldn't it be great if you could keep trees from being killed at all?"

"I've thought of that, too," she quickly replies. She *has* thought this through! "I think we need a rule that says trees can't be cut down to build homes and buildings."

I stand up, excited about her idea. "Do you really think you can get someone to make that rule?"

Danni scrunches her forehead and lets out a sigh, "Probably not. But we could get people to think about what they're doing before bulldozing dozens of trees."

"That would be a good start," I agree. "I'm sure there are other humans as good as you who could help."

"Yes, there must be," Danni nods her head. "Now, we really need to talk about your family. The cloak you found was still in good shape. Maybe your sister lost it right before we found it. Maybe your family is still near the construction site looking for you."

"No, they're not there. I would've felt them if they were."

Danni cocks her head, "Felt them?"

"Yes. It's like the weather thing with our feet. When my family is nearby, I can feel that they are there."

"Oh," Danni says. "So, you think something might have, you know, happened to them?"

"No. I think they made it safely away. I just don't know where they ended up. The cloak was between here and where our tree stood. They must've kept going downstream."

"That's it!" Danni squeals.

Wait, what did I miss? "What's it?"

"Past this neighborhood, there's a wooded area—the Birkhead Wilderness. We should go there and look for them," Danni gets up and pulls out clothes. "I'll get dressed so we can go."

"Danni, who are you talking to?" a voice calls out.

I jump behind the couch and slump down. That has to be Danni's mother.

"No one. Sorry for being so loud," Danni replies. The words "no one" make the tiny hairs on the back of my neck stick out. And not because she yells them, making my ears ring. "I don't like lying to my mom," she whispers. "Maybe someday, I can introduce you to her."

"I don't know, Danni," I say from behind the couch.

"Well, we can talk about that later. Let's go."

The box in the backpack is my seat for the trip. A new magical stick—this one green—lights up the inside of the box. Danni rides her bike past houses. They're all different, but also look the same.

Then, after passing a small house with a big rock chimney, I start to see big, beautiful trees through the periscope tube.

Danni rides a bit farther and then stops to open her backpack. "We're not taking the path. That way, we won't run into any people. Do you want to get on my shoulder?"

"Sure." I dangle my legs off her shoulder and look up at trees so big their branches look like they're shaking hands in the sky. We leave her bicycle against a tree. Then walk into the woods.

The farther we walk, the sadder I feel.

When we can no longer look behind us and see her bike, Danni looks around and asks, "Did you want to look in any of the knotholes in these trees? Do you feel anything?"

"No," I admit. "I don't feel anything." Not my family. Not even other scraebins.

"I'm sorry, Zahra."

We walk farther. Danni steps over logs, moves aside branches, and crosses a stream by stepping on rocks. "Let's take a break. I have some cereal bars and water in my backpack.

We can eat and rest and then walk in another direction."

That's when she realizes she left the backpack attached to her bicycle. "Oh no! I'm so sorry."

"It's okay. We can eat when we get back," I say.

We walk a while longer. At the next stop, we sip water from a creek. While we rest, I close my eyes and try again to feel my family.

"Any luck?" Danni asks.

"No. We can start back. You must be hungry. Maybe we can explore another forest on another day. Are there more forests nearby?"

With a big smile, Danni waves her hands above her head and answers, "This is part of a national forest. It's huge. We can come back and search more. It will take weeks, maybe months to search it all."

Months? A human month is from one full moon to another. I want to find my family now. Not months from now.

Her smile goes away. "I'm sorry Zahra. I don't think it will take that long to find them. I'm sure we'll find your family really soon."

We walk and walk until the sun gets low. No family. No scraebins. And no bike. "I'm really hungry, and my parents are probably worried," Danni finally says.

"Don't you have your phone?" I ask. She always has it with her. "You can call and tell them you're on your way home."

"It's in my backpack. My flashlight is there, too." Danni's eyes dart around. "I don't think I know how to get back. We're lost!"

25

LOST

All day, I concentrated on feeling my family. I was looking for clues. Trying to sense them or other scraebins. I should've focused on helping Danni get back to her bicycle. I point to a cedar tree with two trunks. "That way."

"Are you sure?" Danni asks.

"Yes. The path back is quiet, but I can still feel it," I admit. "Being on your shoulder dulled my senses, but I'm sure. Let's go."

"So you *knew* how to get back this whole time?" Danni's voice is as sharp as a bee's stinger.

"I could've paid more attention and led us back, yes," I squeak out. "I'm sorry, Danni. I was trying to feel something. I just miss them so much."

"I know," she whispers. "It's okay. We're headed back now."

Danni walks and I give directions. We pass the jagged rock formation and she says, "This is right! I remember that." We pass an oak tree that fell across a creek. "And that, too."

"We should make it before the sun sets," I tell her.

"When we get to my bike, I have to call my dad. He's going to have to pick us up."

"Why?" Her father, an adult human, coming to get us is not a good plan.

"There aren't any lights on the road until we get to our neighborhood. It's not safe for me to ride back in the dark. We could get hit by a car," Danni explains. "I'll make sure you're out-of-sight in my backpack."

The sun is halfway gone when we see the bike—and adult humans with flashlights. They're all dressed the same. One is going through her backpack. One has Danni's phone.

"Missed calls from her mother. This is hers, all right," one of them says.

"What's this box for?" another asks as he pulls apart my hideout.

We duck behind a magnolia tree. "Zahra, those are sheriff's deputies," she whispers in a panic. "My parents called the sheriff's office!"

"What are sheriff's deputies?" I ask.

"They protect us. That's what adults always tell me. But . . ." Danni's eyes are filled with tears, and her body is shaking.

"But, what Danni? Will they hurt you?"

She wipes her nose across her sleeve. "No, they won't hurt me. It's just," she takes a deep breath, then swallows hard enough that I have to grip her hair to keep from sliding off her shoulder. "It's just when I was little, and my first mother couldn't take care of me . . . and every time I had to go to a new place to live . . . officers like them were there." She points her chin in the direction of the deputies. "Sometimes, I had to ride with them."

"We're they nice to you?" I ask as I stroke her earlobe.

111

"Mostly, yes. Sometimes they didn't say anything. But there was one who said nice things and gave me a stuffed toy. It's a black poodle with red button eyes. I still have it." Her shoulders stop shaking. She wipes her nose again. "What are we going to do? They'll look for me in the woods. Right here. I need to go out there and let them know I'm okay, but—"

I hop off her shoulder onto the root ball of a dead tree. A cricket scurries away. Danni stares at me, her eyes shifting between mine. "I know," I say. There's nowhere to hide if I go with her. "I'll just stay here. There's plenty for me to eat in the woods, and I can sleep in a tree tonight. I'll search again tomorrow. When it gets dark again, I can fly back."

"Are you sure you're strong enough for all that?" Danni's eyelids are puffy.

"Yes. Now please go over there and let them know you're okay. I'll be fine. Scraebins live in trees in forests just like this." I wave my hand around like I'm giving a tour. "I know how to live out here. This isn't that different from where I used to live with my family."

"But what about the Robins?" she asks.

She's right. They'll be upset. And what if Mrs. Mildred Erdos figures out I'm not in her backyard? "I'm sure they'll understand," I try to sound convincing. "Now go!"

"Please stay safe. And let me know as soon as you're back. Promise?"

"Promise."

Danni rubs her finger down my arm and then scoops me up and sets me on a branch over her head—a nice gesture. She turns and walks toward the humans. One of the deputy officer humans talks into something on his shoulder. He stops when he sees Danni. "Are you Danishia Allman?" he calls to her.

"Yes, sir. I'm so sorry," she replies. Then she begins to sob.

"It's okay," he says. He hands her a bottle of water and puts an arm around her shoulders. "Are you hurt?" He's a nice deputy officer human, like the one that gave her the toy poodle.

"No, sir. I just got lost. I forgot to bring my backpack with me."

"Jeremy, let them know we've got her," he says to one of the other deputy officer humans. Then he turns back to Danni. "What were you doing out here today?"

"I was . . ." she glances in my direction, then looks at the deputy officer human. "Looking for something."

"Your parents said you liked to do science experiments. I'm sure that box in your backpack has something to do with your little adventure."

Danni wipes her face with her sleeve and nods. She looks at the box sticking out of her backpack. The deputy officer human gives her a paper handkerchief. She takes off her spectacles, dries her eyes, and then blows her nose.

"You need to make sure your parents know where you are. And, you never, *ever* come out here to the Birkhead Wilderness without a friend. You're old enough to know about the buddy system, aren't you?" Danni puts her spectacles back on, but doesn't reply. She just hangs her head. "Well, we'll let your parents give you the lecture. And ground you, I'm sure. Let's go."

They give her the phone, put her bike and backpack in the back of one of their cars, and then open a door for her. A few minutes later, the deputy officer humans, all the cars, and Danni are gone.

Lightning bugs light up the forest. Moonlight bounces off shiny, dark green magnolia leaves. Just above me, there's a knothole. Just below, there's a patch of overgrown grass. My stomach is tight. The seeds in the pods balanced at the top of the stalks look delicious. No predators in sight. It's supper time.

I collect seeds, eating one for every two I cram in the fold of my shirt. There's a pool of water in a leaf. It tastes as wonderful as the seeds. Soon, my belly and shirt are full. Other than the sound of crickets, the forest is quiet.

When I get to the knothole, I notice a bigger knothole farther up the tree. It looks like a safer place to sleep, so I keep climbing. A large magnolia bloom blocks the opening. I move it just enough to peek inside. Just behind it, there's furniture.

Then I feel it.

My hands fly to my face. The seeds in my shirt tumble out, bouncing off the bark and splaying across the ground.

There must be a scraebin inside!

26

LONE SCRAEBIN

"Hello?" I call. "Is anyone here?"

To the left I see a stick chair with thick cushions made from yellow and brown tossasides. Next to it is a grayish-purple rock table that's narrow at the bottom and wide and flat on top. The three legs of the table are made with smaller rocks held together with muddy orange clay. To the right, there's a basket woven out of dried grass. It's packed with seeds and nuts. Further back in the shadows is a bed. This must be a scraebin home.

"Well, hello. Welcome."

I swing around and gulp down air. As she steps through a barrier of magnolia blossoms, her long silver hair brushes against the petals. All my senses kick in. My heart is pounding so hard my chest hurts. Sweat drips off my forehead. She *is* a scraebin.

"It is all right, little Zahra. It is wonderful to have you here. Although, I must admit, I did not expect to meet you so soon."

She knows my name, just like Mrs. Mildred Erdos. "Meet me?" I ask. I can hardly catch my breath. Who is this scraebin?

She's not from my colony. Maybe she's from that colony that lived in the pin oak by Danni's house? Maybe she's seen Mother, Father, and Astrael!

"I can see you are distressed. Please sit down." She points to the chair. Then she moves a petal and pulls out another chair. She sits next to me. "Are you hungry?"

"Uhm, no. I just ate." I rub my full stomach.

"Would you like some tea?" she offers.

"No. No, thank you."

She's so beautiful. Her eyes glisten. And they're like mine—a glowing bright shade of amethyst. She's the only other scraebin I've ever seen with amethyst eyes.

"Well, then. I hope you can stay. There is much I must share," she says.

I'm suddenly aware that my mouth is hanging open like the bottom end of a beehive. I snap it shut. What could she possibly need to share with me? And how does she know my name?

"You remind me so much of myself when I was young." She turns and stares at the wall. "That was so long ago."

"Who are you?" I choke out.

She looks back at me. "Oh, of course. You have not developed skills, yet. I am so sorry. You must think me a bit rude. I am sure you understand—a side effect of solitude."

Understand? What is she talking about? She makes less sense than Danni and Mrs. Mildred Erdos. I've been confused since the moment my foot carried me past the magnolia bloom at the door.

"My name is Jellisia Levion. This," she pauses to brush her hand through the air in a semi-circle like I did talking to Danni, "is my home. I have been here for," she looks at the ceiling. "Let me think. This is my second mentor home, so," another pause.

"Fifty-seven — no! Fifty-eight. Yes, fifty-eight years now."

"I'm sorry, but what is a mentor home?" It looks like a normal home to me. Well, except for all the magnolia blossoms. *Those* remind me of Mrs. Mildred Erdos' living room wall. Where are they getting all the fresh blooms so early in spring?

"It is where a mentor lives, young one. That is why I have a bed on the far wall. It is for my trainee. Would you like to see it?" She gets up and moves to the bed. It'd be rude not to follow.

"It looks comfortable," I say. "And warm." The thick blanket is woven with daisy petals.

"I am sure it will be." She smiles and goes back to her chair. "Come sit. Let us talk. I want to know all about you."

From what she's said, I had a feeling she already knew all about me. My stomach is in knots.

"Now, tell me, how did you find me so soon?" she asks.

"So soon? Was I supposed to find you?"

"Of course. But not yet. You are still so young. How old are you? Thirty-seven?"

That she doesn't know? "I'm eleven."

"Eleven! No!" She stands up and throws her hands in the air. "That is just not possible. You cannot be."

"Is that a bad thing?" My eyes dart between her flailing arms and the door.

She drops to her knees and pats my arms. Her hands are soft like Mrs. Robin's under-feathers. "Oh, my young baby. This is much, much too soon. Please tell me, how did you get here?"

I tell her about the Robins and Danni and Mrs. Mildred Erdos. Then I explain about the construction worker humans and how Danni and I were in the forest looking for my family. By the time I get to the part about the deputy officer humans going through Danni's backpack, Miss Jellisia Levion is shaking her head again.

Then silence.

Unsure about asking a question or talking more about the Robins or Mrs. Mildred Erdos, I just stay quiet.

"This is all wrong," she finally says. Miss Jellisia Levion paces around the room. "All wrong. But then, it was bound to happen. What, with all the human encroachment on the forests."

"I'm sorry. I never meant to intrude in your home. We were just looking for my family," I repeat to her. "I know my family is somewhere. I just have to find them."

She looks at me, but doesn't say anything. Instead, she goes outside. While she's gone, I get up and look at the bed. The pillow looks as soft as Miss Jellisia Levion's hands felt. I look out, but don't see or sense her. I step closer to the bed and brush my fingers against the pillow. It's even softer! This would be a wonderful place to spend the night.

"They are fine," Miss Jellisia Levion declares when she pops back in. "Quite close to you, I think. I just cannot pinpoint where." My face turns hot. I pull my hand away from the pillow and scurry to the chair. What must she think of me for touching her things? She sits in her chair. Her hair bounces to one side and falls across her left shoulder and the chair back.

"Who's fine?"

27

A FAIRY

Miss Jellisia Levion looks into my eyes and says, "Your family, of course."

"My family?" I cry out. "You know where they are? Can you help me find them?"

"I wish I could direct you to their exact location, but I cannot stray far. Also, you are going to have to decide whether you *want* to find them."

Her cold words steal the warm picture in my mind of finally finding my family. "Of course, I want to find them. Why wouldn't I?" The streak of a tear burns my cheek. It slips around my chin and onto my neck. My hands ball up.

"My young Zahra, you are different from them. A fact you would have figured out in another thirty or so years. Although, it often takes much longer for a fairy to come to terms with the truth."

"A fairy? Oh, is *that* what you think you are?" My hands unclench. Fairies aren't real. She's been living alone too long. She's confused. When she doesn't answer, I tell her, "Well, I'm not a fairy. I'm a scraebin. And you're a scraebin, too."

"My sweet child, all fairies are scraebins, but not all scraebins are fairies. No one else in your family is likely a fairy. Truthfully, there are very few of us left in the world."

I wipe my face and stand up, stomping my foot and shaking my head. "No! I'm not a fairy. Why are you saying this?"

"I am your mentor."

"My what?" My neck feels like a snake curled up under the summer sun.

"Please, sit down." Her voice is calm, slow, and soft. I sit. "I am your mentor, Zahra. I am supposed to guide you and help develop your skills."

"But I'm not a fairy," I say through gritted teeth. "Fairies don't exist." Then, staring directly into her amethyst eyes, I ask, "Do they?"

"I hope so, because I am a fairy. I have been all my 367 years. Although I did not figure out I was a fairy—or believe, really—until I was 129. My mentor called me a late bloomer."

"See," I point at her, happy to catch her in her lies. "That's impossible. Scraebins only live eighty or ninety years."

She takes a deep breath. So do I.

"Zahra, sweet young Zahra. Scraebins who are not fairies live only eighty or ninety years. Scraebins who are fairies can live more than 900 years. My mentor just marked 1092 years."

My jaw drops.

"You are much too young to transition. This must be overwhelming for you. Please, let me make you tea." She disappears behind a magnolia petal. My ability to sense her vanishes when she leaves the room.

Wait—the magnolia blooms! They must dull the senses. If I'm right, from the looks of this place, Miss Jellisia Levion doesn't want to be found. At least not by scraebins. "Thank you," I say when she hands me steaming tea in the cap of an acorn. It should've been cold. "Do you have a *fire* burning inside this tree?"

"Not at all. That would be disastrous. I would never put a tree in such danger. Nor the forest."

Staring at her, I challenge, "Then how did you warm my tea?"

"You will see. It is a skill. But not one you will have for quite some time." She sits down with her tea and takes a sip. "Now, go ahead. Ask me your questions."

Is she able to read my mind? Can she see all the questions bouncing in my head?

"It is your expression. And my heightened senses. Now ask. I am listening."

So, she *is* reading my mind! But that can't be. She takes another sip. She's waiting for me to say something. A question bubbles up through the confusion. "It makes me sad to think—if I *am* a fairy—that I'll have to lose my parents and my sister. And everyone I've ever known. Even Danni. Why would anyone *want* to be a fairy?"

"No one wants to be a fairy. You just either are a fairy, or you are not. Now what else?" She takes another sip.

"Why did you say I have to decide whether or not I want to go back to my family?" I can feel tears pushing up to my eyes.

"My, you are an emotional fairy. I do not know if this is unusual, or if it is just because you are so young," she says. There's another long pause before she finally gives me an answer. "Scraebins who are not fairies are taught not to believe in fairies. So much so that they become cross at the mere suggestion that fairies exist."

I suppose that makes sense. But I'm not convinced. Maybe she's just unwell. Really, 367 years old? She hardly looks as old as Mother. And Mother is only thirty-six.

She puts her tea down and continues, "Your family may not believe you're a fairy. If they do, they might not want you to stay with their colony."

That's a terrible thing to say. "They'd never kick me out. They love me."

"Of course they do," Miss Jellisia Levion agrees. "But scraebins naturally ostracize fairies. It is in their DNA. It is a protective mechanism."

"What's ostracize? And protective mechanism? And why?" The questions come easier with every answer she gives.

She explains that because fairies live so long and there are so few of them, it's best for scraebins and fairies to live apart. Scraebins don't understand the skills or sharp senses—much sharper than even the most sensitive scraebins—of fairies. A scraebin who is a fairy doesn't usually find out until they are much, much older. Miss Jellisia Levion's family and friends had all passed away before she found her mentor. By then, she'd even lost touch with her grandnephew—her only living relative. She explains that not all fairies are mentors. While in training, each fairy discovers their purpose.

When she finally stops talking, there's one more question itching my brain. "That bed." I look toward the back wall. "It's mine, isn't it?"

"Yes." She nods. "It is." She smiles the way Miss Evelie Poeley did when I answered a question correctly. "I made it especially for you. Although, when I began building it, I thought I would have many years to complete the work. Two full moons ago, I was consumed by urgency. It had to be done at once. I finished it only this morning."

She collects our acorn caps and disappears again. When she

returns, she says, "You must be exhausted. I think it is time for you to try out your new bed."

When I told Danni I'd curl up in a knothole for the night, I never imagined I'd get to sleep on the softest pillow ever made under a daisy petal blanket in the house of a scraebin who thinks she's a fairy.

28

HEART ANIMALS

The smell of warmed seeds tickles my nose. It feels like I'm curled up in a cloud. My whole body is strong and full of energy. The early songs of birds make me feel happy deep inside—a happy I haven't felt since I lost my family.

Birds? Oh no! My arms pop up and knock the seeds off the table next to the bed. The Robins must be terribly worried.

"How do you feel this morning?" Miss Jellisia Levion holds a steaming cup of tea. Ignoring the scattered seeds, she puts the tea on the table.

"Just wonderful," I say, jumping to the floor to scoop up my mess. When the seeds are back in an acorn cap, I walk to the table and plop down on a chair. "But I *am* a little—"

"Worried," she cuts me off. "I know. The robins will be fine."

"*How* do you know? And why do I feel so well? Is it because living in the birdhouse was bad for me, and I'm finally healthy again after sleeping in a tree in the forest?"

"I realize you have lots more questions. I am sure you know that it is more than a night in a tree that has you so spry. I am guessing you cannot remember a time when you felt this well or strong."

I want to believe I'm feeling great because of the tree. But she's right. I feel better than I've ever felt in my entire life. "Eat, and then you can change into some fresh clothes." She looks at my bed. The covers are neatly pulled into place. Draped across it is a silky white dress with pink petals around the middle.

"How did—"

"I will answer your questions after breakfast. Now eat."

Every bite dances on my tongue with the most wonderful flavors. Even the tea is fruitier and brighter than anything I've tasted, including my parents' blackberry pecan stew. I offer to help clear the table, but Miss Jellisia Levion insists I change my clothes.

"Come, we can sit atop the tree and talk," she says as soon as I'm dressed.

We fly—which feels more like drifting—to the highest branch of the magnolia tree. I look around as we float higher. No blooms. It's too early. She has to be getting them from somewhere. When we reach the top, there are crooks in the branch that form two seats.

"It's beautiful up here," I say, looking out over the trees. "I can see Danni's neighborhood." There's no way to tell which house is which, but there's one roof that looks like it might be Danni's.

"This visit may become too overwhelming for you. Whenever you want to go back inside to rest, please let me know. Until then, we can start with you asking another question." There are so many questions that it's hard to decide what to ask. As if she's still reading my mind, she suggests, "Take a deep breath and then focus. What is nagging at you the most?"

By the time I exhale, it comes to me. "Do you use magnolia blossoms to hide from other scraebins? It feels like they dull my senses."

"Excellent question. But no, actually. Fairies seek out places to live that are devoid of scraebins. These days, it is not hard." She tells me that magnolia blossoms do calm the senses. Fairies—she's still adamant that we *are* fairies—are extra-sensitive. They feel everything, all the time, which can be hard on the body. By filling her home with magnolia blossoms, she's able to shield her body from the outside world. It allows her to fully rest at night and wake up strong and energized in the morning.

"Where do you find fresh magnolia blossoms? It's too early for them to bloom. And the ones you have are pure white without any brown edges."

Miss Jellisia Levion smiles. "You are certainly observant. And perceptive. I gather blooms that I coaxed from the tree. Coaxing is a skill. Fairies are able to coax magnolias to produce blooms. This can be done year round."

"Do you get up early each day or stay up at night to coax new blooms?" I ask.

"Not at all. Coaxed blooms stay fresh, white, and fragrant for at least three moons."

I feel my eyes grow wide the way Danni's always do. "Why don't they teach us about magnolia blossoms and coaxing in school? Wouldn't that be helpful to all scraebins?"

"Scraebins are not sensitive enough to need magnolia blossoms. Of course, by comparison, scraebins are much more sensitive than humans and many of the creatures that roam the Earth. Fairies, however, are born much more sensitive. This sensitivity only deepens as they are trained."

She also reminds me that scraebins don't have fairy skills, so there's no need to make them aware of coaxing, which they can't do. And while her story explains her magnolia blooms, it doesn't tell me why Mrs. Mildred Erdos' parlor wall is covered in what must be coaxed blooms. Unless Mrs. Mildred Erdos is *also* a fairy.

"Why would a human have fresh magnolia blossoms covering an entire wall in her home?"

"My little one, humans like to decorate. They can be frivolous. There could be many reasons why a human would use them. My question back to you is how would you know what a human has in its home? Did you go into your friend Danni's house?"

I have an awful feeling that going into a human's house is not a good idea for fairies. Or scraebins. Or scraebins who are supposed to be fairies and just met their mentor—*if* any of this is actually real. Rather than ask another question, I tell her about visiting Danni's room and having tea with Mrs. Mildred Erdos.

"She is a Sentinelian. Yours, I am guessing," she says

"So you know about the Society of the Sentinelia?" I ask. But then, as an adult scraebin, of course she would know.

"Yes, young one. They, too, are dissipating in numbers. I never thought it was a good idea to create the Society. My mentor's mentor was an elder-fairy when the decision was made. Every 100 years, the program is re-evaluated. I have weighed in twice now. Sentinelia like your Mrs. Mildred Erdos are giving me plenty of reason to continue to speak against its continuation. But that is a story for another time. What else do you want to know?"

A story for another time? I want to know what Mrs. Mildred

Erdos is doing wrong now. But rather than push her to go on—the way her face looks makes it clear she isn't going to say any more about it—I come up with another question that might help me understand. "Can Mrs. Mildred Erdos coax blooms, too?"

Miss Jellisia Levion looks into the distance, takes in a deep breath, and then lets it out slowly. "Some Sentinelia can." Her lips are tight, and lines appear above her eyes.

It's time to change the subject. "I'd like it very much if my sister could be a fairy," I state as I look out in the direction of Danni's roof.

"That was not a question. And I am sure you understand that you are either born a fairy or you are not."

"What about cats? Are fairies friends with cats?"

Miss Jellisia Levion lets out a laugh. At least she's not frowning anymore. "You must be referring to Gigesdi," she says.

I turn and look at her. "You know *her*, too?"

"She is one of your heart animals. I am surprised she has already made herself known to you."

Every answer she gives creates more questions. It's like a flower that changes as its petals open. "Heart animal? What's a heart animal?"

Miss Jellisia Levion explains that all fairies have a team of heart animals that help them. Gigesdi must have sensed me as soon as she was weaned from her mother. She says it's not unheard of, but for a heart animal to connect with its fairy so early is especially unusual. It must be because of my 'special circumstances.'

Before I ask Miss Jellisia Levion to explain my 'special circumstances,' another question pops into my head. "You said fairies have a team of heart animals—so, more than one. Will I have others?" It'd be great if there weren't any heart owls or heart mountain lions. A cat is scary enough.

"Of course," she answers as if I already knew.

"And will they all have amethyst eyes?" That would make it much easier to tell whether an animal is a threat or part of my team when one shows up out of nowhere.

"You are so ahead of your time, young Zahra. Yes, all of yours have amethyst eyes," she answers. Then she points. "Look over there at the water. That is the stream that rushes past where you live. Can you see the amethyst rocks?" I lean toward the stream, trying hard to focus on the exact spot her finger points. There are four, no . . . five rocks the same color as my eyes. It's almost as if the sun is reflecting off just those five rocks.

"There are seven rocks," she says.

I squint my eyes and scan the spot, trying to see what she sees. "I only see five."

"That is because you only see the ones at the very top. Life is deeper than what you see on the surface. You will learn and hone your skills in time. And you will be able to see much more than what most notice."

I think she's talking about more than just rocks. "Why are there seven?" I ask.

"You have seven heart animals. Although, they may not all be born yet."

My mind is a jumble of confusion. "But if I'm supposed to live hundreds of years, what happens when they die?"

"Take a breath, young one. Listen to the wind," she answers. She puts her arm on my shoulder and says, "Then you tell me."

I close my eyes, fill my lungs with air, and listen. The answer is in my heart. It's so simple. "They live as long as I do, don't they?"

Miss Jellisia Levion smiles.

29

BLUE EGGS

T he sun is barely up when I get back to the Robins'
house. My stomach is tight. I just know they'll be
upset I was away so long, even if they are happy to see
me. I'll be grounded for sure.

Mr. Robin is sitting at the door. His body blocks my way
into the birdhouse.

"I'm home, Mr. Robin. I'm so sorry for being away." He
doesn't budge. He looks angry. "May I come in?" I try to step
around him, but he flaps a wing and nudges me away from the
door. "Mr. Robin, please. It's me, Zahra. I know I'm wearing
different clothes. But it *is* me."

There's a chirp from behind him. He turns to Mrs. Robin
and squawks. I cover my ears at the sharp sound. She answers
with another soft chirp.

He steps aside.

Mrs. Robin isn't tidying the birdhouse or arranging twigs.
Instead, she's sitting on her nest. Her body is spread out so it
takes the whole space. And she looks different. She doesn't
get up to hug me. Instead, she moves just a bit and turns her

head. Not sure what to think, I close my eyes, take a breath, and listen. Maybe taking a moment works for more than just learning about heart animals. I let out a breath, and my heart fills with joy.

An egg!

"Do you have a brand new egg, Mrs. Robin?"

She chirps.

"Of course! Oh, but now I feel worse about being away so long. I'm sorry I made you both worry."

I scurry to my room, slip my arms into Astrael's cloak, and curl up in my nest. The trip home should've been exhausting. Instead, I feel great. All that Miss Jellisia Levion told me repeats in my head. Questions pile up like oak catkins in spring.

Am I really a fairy? Will I live hundreds of years? If my family is nearby, why can't I feel them? If Miss Jellisia Levion is a mentor fairy, why can't she use her skills to tell me *exactly* where my parents and Astrael are?

There is so much I don't understand. I'm not sure Danni will believe any of this. Can I even tell Danni? There's no way around the truth that Danni's a human. Scraebins are not supposed to go inside humans' houses.

But there's no one else to tell. With all that she's already done and already knows, I just have to tell her. That's when I remember with a slap to my forehead—I already told Danni fairies don't exist.

Another breath and quiet moment. My thoughts settle. Like a forest after the morning mist burns away, everything becomes clear. It's simple.

I *will* tell Danni everything. She's my best friend. She's a human, but she's not dangerous. We will find my family. They might not understand at first, but they love me. They will find a way to accept me—assuming I *am* a fairy.

One more breath.

The wind is soft. My heart flutters. *Am* I a fairy?

* * *

After all the changes over the last day—including another egg in the Robins' nest—it's nice to be in Danni's room again. I can't wait to tell her about Miss Jellisia Levion.

But first, she tells me about being grounded. Her parents even took away her phone. When the deputy officer humans brought her home, her parents were standing at the door. They were terrified. And disappointed. And frustrated.

"I can't really blame them," Danni says. "I was difficult when they were my foster parents. I ran away seven times. One time, I even bit my dad's leg just to get away. I didn't even know where I was going. I was barely five. I just didn't trust them. It still doesn't make sense sometimes—why they adopted me after all that."

"They must really love you," I say.

"They sure do—enough to take my phone for a whole month, according to my mom. And I can't go out, either. Not even in the backyard. Which means I can't," Danni hangs her head. "I can't help you find your parents."

"That won't be a problem, Danni. I'm sure they're not far from here."

Her head pops up, and so do her eyebrows. "How do you know? What happened last night? And where did you get that beautiful new dress?"

After her story about being grounded, it's good to hear her firing off a bunch of questions with a spark in her eyes. I

133

explain about the knothole and the magnolia blossoms. Then I describe Miss Jellisia Levion as best I can, although Danni looks skeptical when I get to the part about her age. "So what you're saying is," she says, stretching out her words. Here it comes. "You *are* a fairy! I just knew it!"

My eyes roll so hard my head aches. My hands want to ball up, but they stay limp in my lap. Like it or not, I'm starting to believe I really am a fairy. When Danni finally gets over her excitement, I explain about Miss Jellisia Levion feeling a sense of my family.

"So, she knows where they are?" Danni asks.

"Not exactly. She felt them near here, but she couldn't tell me exactly where. She was sure they're alive and well, though."

"Oh Zahra, that's wonderful! I wish I could help you find them," Danni says.

It won't be easy without her. Gigesdi can protect me, but we could do so much more *and* save time if Danni could help.

After a deep breath, I listen.

The answer pops into my head. "You still can," I say. "We can plan together. You can help me draw a map that will make sure I cover all the trees and hidden places in all our neighbors' yards."

Danni pulls out paper and pencils before I finish telling her my idea. "We'll make a map, and a plan, and you'll report back each evening," she says. "Then we can review what you've covered and update the plan."

We whisper so Danni's parents don't hear us. We have to quiet a few giggles along the way. By the time we finish, Danni has a lot written on her notepad, including a very nice drawing of our neighborhood. We color the map together.

That night, only one thought nags at me. If I really *am*

supposed to live hundreds of years, it's going to be awfully lonely for all the ones that don't include Danni.

30

OVERNIGHT VISIT

My first job is to get past the magnolia tree on the other side of Mrs. Mildred Erdos' backyard. From there, I'll report back to Danni with more places to explore.

There are buds all over the old gnarled tree. Ivy climbs the trunk and hugs the underside of its lower branches. Some of those branches are nearly as big as the trunk. The ground is covered with overgrown clumps of grass, shiny brown decaying leaves, and pods with soft fibers pushing out of the tips.

I'm wearing my old clothes instead of the silky dress Miss Jellisia Levion gave me. The old clothes help me blend in, which is important since it's a sunny day. Walking helps save energy. I'll need to fly back in case of an emergency—like a hawk attack or if Mrs. Mildred Erdos' other neighbor lets their little boy out to play.

Danni said the boy is three years old and curious. He's also rough with his toys. She said she helped babysit him once. He pulled the head off a plastic toy dog, ripped the stuffing out of a pillow, and threw a ball into a lamp. She doesn't help babysit him anymore.

The rocks, overgrown grass, and leaves make it hard to walk fast, especially while keeping watch for humans and scary animals. There are also spider webs. I decide it's better to wait on Gigesdi for help. I sit down on a magnolia cone and close my eyes.

I breathe in and think of Gigesdi. I have no idea how she always finds me. There's no way for me to find her. But if she's my heart animal, she must know when I'm thinking of her. Maybe if she senses me thinking of her, she will know to come. My idea makes as much sense as me being a fairy, so I go with it.

Breathe in. Thoughts of Gigesdi.

Breathe out. Thoughts of Gigesdi.

Breathe in. Thoughts of Gigesdi.

Breathe out.

SNAP!

A twig breaks. Then footsteps. Heavy footsteps.

My eyes fly open. Mrs. Mildred Erdos is waddling toward me, her long braid swinging from side to side. She was *not* in my thoughts, but she *is* outside. And she's headed right for this magnolia tree.

"My goodness, she's a bold one," she says to the sky. Then she barks, "What are you doing out here where the neighborhood can see you? There's a little boy that lives just next door. He's not old enough to be in school, but he *is* old enough to not only see you, but also pick you up and bite your head off!" Mrs. Mildred Erdos bends down, scoops me up, and then drops me in one of her apron pockets.

I freeze. What do I do? We swing around and I catch a

glimpse of Gigesdi. Now she shows up? Mrs. Mildred Erdos stomps up the steps, across the back porch, and then into her kitchen.

SLAM!

She crashes the door closed. If Gigesdi was right behind us, the door would've knocked her back across the porch and into the yard.

"What's the matter?" I blurt out. "This can't be just because I was outside during the day. Is something else wrong? Was I in danger?"

"I'm getting much too old for this, Herbert," she says to the ceiling. "Something is wrong. Something is very, very wrong. What were you up to out there?"

Mrs. Mildred Erdos puts me on her kitchen table. Without waiting for my answer, she stomps off to the living room. She returns with a chair for me. I sit down, and she makes tea. "Well? Why did I find you under my magnolia tree?" she asks, clanging cups and spoons and other human kitchen things.

She won't like the truth, so I think of something else. "I . . . I was looking for something."

"You already know, don't you?" she snaps.

"Know what?" I ask.

She could be talking about the fairy thing. Maybe it's about my family? Is there something else?

She shakes her head. She hands me warm rosehip hibiscus tea in an acorn cap, just like Miss Jellisia Levion. "I know, I know," she says to the window. Then she pours herself a cup. "I think you should spend the night, Miss Zahra. You should spend the night, and we should get to know each other. Maybe two nights. It might take that long."

My hand shakes. Tea spills on my leg. It makes a deep pink

spot. "Thank you, but I don't think so. I really need to get back to the Robins." I try to wipe the tea off my skirt.

"They're just fine. And they're expecting. I suspect by tomorrow, there will be three eggs in that nest. Then, all of their focus will be on hatching those babies. No room for you anymore."

My head drops. I love the Robins. They love me. Why wouldn't they have room for me? The babies will be small. They'll sleep in the nest with them.

"It's how it should be. They are birds. You need to be—"

"With my family!" I cut her off.

"Humph. I was going to say with me. I *am* your family. At least for now. I suppose I could build you your own wooden house. We could move that nest bed of yours into it. That might work, don't you think, Herbert?"

"I don't want to live alone. And I really must be going. There are plenty of knotholes in the trees by the stream. Staying here will—"

"Be just fine. See, I can cut people off mid-sentence, too. This house was made from fallen trees. I keep fresh logs by the fireplace along with the dried logs. You can sleep there. You'll be fine."

Danni expects me to report back tonight. She'll worry if I don't show up. But Mrs. Mildred Erdos won't listen. And she sounds so angry. "I'll just finish my tea and then go back to the birdhouse and grab a couple of things," I say as I stand up. Of course, my plan is to *stay* outside once I leave.

"I've got spare clothes, a comfortable bed, warm blankets, and plenty of food. What else could you possibly need?"

A way to escape comes to mind.

Flying was a possibility after she plopped me in her pocket, but I couldn't move. I was scared and surprised. That can't be very fairy-like. It's not even scraebin-like.

Maybe Miss Jellisia Levion was wrong about me and my heart cat. I sit back down and look out the window. Gigesdi is walking back and forth along the rail on the back porch. Mrs. Mildred Erdos doesn't notice her. If she did, she'd go after her with a broom again.

31

NO WAY OUT

The clothes she pulls out of an apron pocket feel rough and dry. Not that I'm going to wear them. They aren't in my hands more than the blip of a hungry toad's tongue before I set them down to check my hands for scratches. She probably made them out of black walnut husks. Or maybe they've been in her pocket as long as she's lived here. Either way, compared to my shimmery, silky dress from Miss Jellisia Levion, wearing these clothes would be like wrapping myself in bark from an old oak tree.

"You can wear those tomorrow. You should be fine to sleep in your clothes tonight, even with that tea stain," Mrs. Mildred Erdos says. Then she looks up. "Although, she could probably sleep in just her shirt, don't you think, Herbert? That magnolia petal blanket is quite warm."

"Is that why you have so many magnolia leaves on that wall?" I ask, pointing at the front door.

She squints, "What did you say?"

"Do you keep magnolia blossoms to make blankets?" She doesn't blink or move, so I ask more questions, "Is that one of your responsibilities?" She's so still, I'm not sure she's breathing. "As a Sentinelian?"

"We are not spending our time discussing my décor!" Mrs. Mildred Erdos finally snaps back. Then she stomps back to the kitchen.

She makes so much tea, I'm starting to believe that maybe, if it were possible, she's part scraebin. Maybe all the time she spent protecting scraebins made her like us. Then again, making tea with hot water is a human thing.

While clacking around the kitchen, she describes the neighborhood and how, when she and Mr. Herbert Erdos found this spot, there were no wasteful houses around. There was only the forest. They built this log cabin from fallen trees, clay, and stones they gathered with their own two hands. When she returns with our tea, I'm ready for more stories about her life here with Mr. Herbert Erdos.

"Now, let's talk about you, shall we?" she sings out, holding a pot of lavender chamomile tea. She already knows where I live—she put me there. She knows my family is lost. She knows I want to find them. There's not much more to tell. At least, not to her. "Tell me more about Miss Danishia." She pours the tea. "I'd love to know what draws you to her."

"Oh, she is my—" I stop myself before it comes out. Danni's my best friend. But that's not something Mrs. Mildred Erdos needs to hear, especially since she doesn't trust Danni. I look around the room and then back at Mrs. Mildred Erdos. She's supposed to protect me. But I don't feel safe here like I do with Danni or the Robins.

"She's your what, my dear?" she asks. "Please, go on."

My leg is moving. I put my hand down to stop it. As fancy as her scraebin-sized human chair is, it's not as comforting as the furniture in Miss Jellisia Levion's home. "I was just going to say that she is my age." I take a breath before continuing. "I thought it would be good for me to learn about humans from one that's young like me."

"Is that right?" she asks. "What do you think, Herbert? Yes. We should let her sleep. Maybe she'll make more sense in the morning." Mrs. Mildred Erdos clears our tea cups. Then she disappears down a hallway into a room. Her bedroom.

As soon as the moon rises past the top of the window, I go to the kitchen. Danni's waiting for my report. Tonight, I want to sleep in my nest. Tomorrow, I want to wear my new dress again, not the scratchy clothes from Mrs. Mildred Erdos' apron pocket.

The window over the sink is the first place I check. It's closed and locked. I push the latch with all my might, but it doesn't move. The door is no help, either. It's shut up tighter than the cap of an early acorn in late summer.

There has to be a way out of this house. I need to calm down so I can come up with a plan. That's what Danni would do—stop and figure out how to solve the problem. Too bad I don't have a pencil and notepad. Or know how to read or write human words.

Perched on the logs next to the fireplace—the new ones, not the dried ones—my head clears after a few long breaths. There are other windows to check. And the front door.

Part of me wants to inspect each of them and then check the timber walls for holes. The house is old. I'm guessing since Mr. Herbert Erdos' death, it's been more difficult for Mrs. Mildred Erdos to take care of the house all alone.

Another part of me feels scared—as if nothing I try will work, and I'll end up draining my body.

More breaths.

A tear spills down my cheek. I don't want to be stuck here.

Against the strongest feelings gnawing at my heart, I fly to each window and then the front door. Nothing will budge. I go to the walls and crawl up and down. I feel for cracks or holes. But there's nothing.

Finally, exhausted, I climb onto the sappier logs in the pile and curl up in the magnolia petal blanket. That's when it hits me like a frosty chunk of hail.

Mrs. Mildred Erdos kidnapped me!

My chest feels like it's filled with wet moss. My heart aches for Mother. I want to fall asleep in her warm arms and wake up around my family. Instead, I'm wedged in a pile of logs in the home of a human who's supposed to be protecting me, but may have lost her mind long before my family's tree was destroyed. She probably doesn't like Danni because Danni is kind and good and would protect me from being kidnapped.

With a wet face, I get a little sleep—and only because I'm so tired. When the first light of morning pushes through the kitchen window, my wings are strong enough to carry me to the highest shelf on the front wall. That's where I hide wrapped in a magnolia blossom.

32

IN THE CABIN

The blossoms on the shelves and door are fresh like the ones in Miss Jellisia Levion's house. Mrs. Mildred Erdos must be good at coaxing magnolias. I'm glad. The soft petals are like a hug. They also give me a place to hide so I can figure out what to do.

By now, the Robins and Danni must be worried. They probably think I was caught by a wild animal or the baby human that lives next door. They'll never guess I'm trapped inside the house of a human who's supposed to protect scraebins—or that she kidnapped me.

"This is odd. You didn't change into fresh clothes," Mrs. Mildred Erdos says as she walks into the living room. The scratchy outfit is still folded next to the logs. "Where are you, Zahra? In the kitchen? An early riser, maybe?" She shuffles away. Cabinets open and close. She returns to the living room. "Zahra, enough now! I know you're here. It's time for breakfast," she calls out. Then she looks up. "Why must this one be so difficult, Herbert?"

She looks right at the shelf. She must've seen me when she

was talking to Mr. Herbert Erdos. Or maybe I moved a petal. I freeze, barely able to breathe.

"Come down from there, Zahra. You could get hurt!"

Other than her, there's nothing in the room that can hurt me. Unless she has an owl or snake hidden in a closet. She goes to the kitchen to make breakfast. My stomach wants me to follow. I wonder if there's a fairy skill that could make it so I can walk through the wall to the outside. Unsure what to do, I don't move. Crouched in this blossom is the safest I've felt since she kidnapped me, yesterday.

"Mashed banana and warm black tea to start the day," she sings. My stomach creaks like an old tree during a spring thunderstorm. "Oh, look! Leftover acorn soup. She might like that too, don't you think, Herbert?"

Deep breath. Food will help me keep my strength up, which I need to find a way out. I can keep lots of space between her hands and me.

"Nice of you to fly over and join us," she says as I slide the scraebin-sized chair and table as far away from where she sits as possible. "Be careful! You don't want to spill your meal," she snaps.

During breakfast, she talks about the 'old days' when scraebins appreciated the help of the Society of the Sentinelia. Scraebins rarely came inside back then. There was no need. There were plenty of trees. There were also lots of colonies with fewer humans to interfere. She mostly says 'people' instead of humans. As I eat and listen, I begin to wonder if she likes humans at all—other than Herbert, of course.

"Have you always been a Sentinelian?"

"Oh dear, no." Her eyes get wide. "But I can't remember a time when I didn't know about them."

"How did you know?" I ask. Danni is human and she didn't know.

"My grandmother was part of the Society," Mrs. Mildred Erdos says as she looks out the window. "I loved spending time with her. She had the most beautiful gardens. I spent hours just wandering through her sunflowers, tulip beds, and butterfly bushes. That's where I met Juniper."

"Who's Juniper?" I ask, keeping my eyes on her even as I shovel scoops of mashed banana into my mouth. It's sweet and delicious.

"She was my best friend in the world. My only friend, actually." She pauses for a sip of tea. Her eyes droop.

I stop chewing. "What happened to her?"

"Oh, she died of a broken heart, poor thing." Another pause. "But that was long ago. So very long ago. Long before I met my Herbert."

"That's terrible. Did she lose her husband, too?"

One corner of Mrs. Mildred Erdos' mouth slides down. "No, no. She never married. No, Juniper fell ill mourning the death of her mother. It was a horrible tragedy, what happened to her mother."

"You don't have to tell me." Looking at Mrs. Mildred Erdos' face, I don't think I want to know. "I'm sorry. I didn't mean to make you sad."

"Oh, no. I need to tell you. That's why you're here. You need to know how horrible people can be. Outside of the Society, people are terrible. Just awful."

Mrs. Mildred Erdos needs to learn that some humans *are* good. But she's not going to listen to me. She nibbles bits of her food. Then she sighs and tells me the story of Juniper's mother—they were scraebins—getting caught in a dish of honey outside a house. The humans who lived there were shocked to find her. They'd never seen a scraebin. They decided to put her in a glass jar and keep her on a shelf.

Their plan was to make money by charging other people to see her. Back then, before books, radios, televisions, or flashy phones like Danni's, she says people paid other people to see odd things. Like an animal with an extra leg. Or a very tiny person with the legs of a frog, which is what Mrs. Mildred Erdos said the humans thought she was. They called her The Mini Frog Woman. But before they ever made one piece of money, Juniper's mother died in the jar.

It was just like Miss Evelie Poeley told us. I push my plate away.

Mrs. Mildred Erdos tells me one would think this tragedy would've upset the people who captured Juniper's mother. But it didn't bother them at all. They decided a dead tiny person with frog legs was as good as a live one.

Late one night, before the people could charge others to see the body of The Mini Frog Woman, and while everyone slept, Juniper's mother's body disappeared. It was the work of a Sentinelian.

All I can say is "That's so awful. I'm sorry."

"Take heed, my dear. People are not to be trusted," Mrs. Mildred Erdos says while pointing her finger at me.

The image of Juniper's dead mother will be hard to forget. Even though it was a horrible story, I tell her, "Not *all* humans are bad." But my voice is shaky.

"Well, when I meet one outside of the Society that's good, I'll let you know," she replies. Then she spreads strawberry jam on a piece of bread and takes a bite.

My heart feels sad for Mrs. Mildred Erdos. Danni proves

there are humans with good hearts. After that story, though, I'm sure I'll never be able to get Mrs. Mildred Erdos to believe it. She'll never listen to a scraebin, especially one that's a child.

"I'd like to go home now," I finally say. She must feel bad for me after remembering Juniper's mother. "I'm sure the Robins are worried."

"They're occupied with their eggs, now," she replies. "They're fine. Go change your clothes and I'll give you the full tour of my home."

Putting on those scratchy clothes sounds terrible, but I don't want to anger Mrs. Mildred Erdos. If I'm stuck here, I might as well learn as much about the house as possible. That way tonight, if she still hasn't set me free, I'll be able to find a way out.

33

ESCAPE

It's a long day of Mrs. Mildred Erdos and her stories as we go through the five rooms in her cabin. There are many shelves on the walls. Lots of things are made of rock, wood, moss, and flowers that she and Mr. Herbert Erdos collected on their land. She has a whole shelf of scraebin-sized furniture and dishes. Many of her shelves are packed with dusty old books. Most of the books, she says, are her journals. When we're in the room she calls a library, she tells me she's written in a journal every day since the moment she became a Sentinelian.

Besides all the books, the front walls of the cabin—in both the living room and the library—are covered in fresh magnolia blossoms.

"What do you use all the magnolia blooms for?" I ask her during a pause in one of her stories. That's when she decides we need lunch. Sipping tea and nibbling acorn cakes, I realize she never answered my question about the magnolias. I'm also no closer to finding a way out. I tried twice to ask why we had to stay inside. I even suggested we eat outside on her back porch. Instead of answering me, she just kept looking up and telling Mr. Herbert Erdos that I was a handful. She even called me sassy two more times.

During supper, I ask her how old she is. Her eyes wander away from me to the walls. Then a tear falls down her cheek. After a long silence, she finally says, "A lady doesn't ask about or tell her age." Then she gets up to light candles. The candles are everywhere. She makes them. I don't like candles. All I can picture is fire spreading through the whole house with us in it. My whole body shivers.

Mrs. Mildred Erdos' cabin isn't anything like Danni's house. The only electric light is in the big food cabinet in the kitchen—the refrigerator.

After supper, we talk a little while longer. Mostly she talks. She tells me how lucky I am to have her watching out for me. She tells me scraebins without Sentinelia live in fear, which I find hard to believe since I wasn't afraid when I didn't know about Sentinelia. She also assures me that in her home, I'm safe.

I don't feel safe.

Before two drips slide down the side of the candle on the table, she says it's bedtime. "When the sun goes down, we need to follow soon after," she tells me. Then she blows out all the candles, which makes me feel better—until I cough from the tails of smoke that dance above the melted wax.

By the time Mrs. Mildred Erdos closes her bedroom door, I realize I'm still wearing the clothes that felt so itchy. But they're not itchy. They're comfortable. And there's a new set piled next to the freshest logs on the hearth. Mrs. Mildred Erdos is an odd human. As much as I try, I just don't understand her.

More deep breaths. She could be a threat. She might also be

a good person.

My heart and mind don't agree. They're flip-flopping like a squirrel that doesn't know whether to cross a path or return to where it started.

Deep breaths. In. Out.

The first strong thought that pops into my mind is *Gigesdi*. My eyes fly open. There she is!

"How did you get in?" I whisper. Gigesdi scampers over and rubs her head against the side of my body. Wait—if she was able to get in, I can get out!

Gigesdi leans down. I change into my own clothes and leave Mrs. Mildred Erdos' scraebin clothes next to the logs. After settling on Gigesdi's back, we creep into the library. Under the lowest shelf on the front wall, Gigesdi pushes a floor plank with her front paws. One side of the plank goes up while she pushes on the half that goes down. I duck, and we jump into the darkness underneath the wall.

The moment we slip under the house, my senses come alive.

Mother? Father? Astrael? But there's no one around.

Gigesdi makes her way to a hole in the rock wall that holds up the cabin. The moon is bright. The trees, leaves, grass, pinecones, breeze, rushing water—it all fills my senses. But the biggest feeling shooting through my body is one that tells me my family is here.

Tears sting my eyes. My heart pounds hard against my ribs.

Gigesdi hops onto the front porch of the cabin. In the corner, a stout magnolia tree grows through the floorboards. That's where they are, I just know it. I sense it in every part of my body.

At the base of the tree, Gigesdi kneels down. I grab the rough bark and climb. The higher I climb, the more I feel not only my family, but also other scraebins. It's overwhelming. It *has* to be my colony.

Halfway up the trunk, terrible thoughts stop me.

What if I get to the knothole and my family isn't there? What if they are, and they really don't want me like Miss Jellisia Levion said? My hands are wet with sweat. My mind races. If my family and my colony are here, Mrs. Mildred Erdos didn't have to put me in a birdhouse with the Robins. So, why did she?

Every ridge of bark feels rough on my fingers and toes. Moonlight bounces off leaves, windows, rocks, and the tips of the waves in the stream. Crickets chirp, a human car drives past, a toad croaks. The scent of dew and earth twitches my nostrils. The fishy taste of lichen settles on my tongue as I breathe.

It's. All. Too. Much.

"Mother!" I cry out as I cling to the bark below the knothole.

Frozen.

Terrified.

Excited.

Confused.

"Zahra?" a small voice above my head calls.

"Mother!" I swallow hard and try to take a deep breath, but I still can't move.

"Berniad! Astrael! Come quick. Our Zahra! It's her!"

Shadows scurry out of the knothole.

Darkness.

* * *

My eyes flutter open. My head is on a pillow. Mother and

153

Father stand above me. Astrael strokes my hair.

I can't speak. Tears stream down my cheeks.

"The world is good and kind. I have my Zahra back," Mother says. "Are you hungry, my baby? I have stew. Your favorite."

My eyes give Mother her answer. She disappears. She soon returns with the most delicious stew I've ever tasted.

"What made you decide to come back?" Mother asks.

34

FAMILY REUNION

Mother and Father tell me about the horrible day the construction worker humans destroyed our tree. There are others from our colony living in Mrs. Mildred Erdos' magnolia. Most of the colony headed west to the thick, old forests in the big mountains. Astrael lost her cloak when she tried to find me, but then had to rush back to Mother and Father after a hawk dove at her. A chill shakes my shoulders as I picture her escaping death. My family hid until dark in the bank of the river—I mean stream—with those who didn't leave. Then they flew across the stream to this tree.

As I watch and listen to my family, something doesn't feel right.

"Why did you ask me what made me decide to come back?" I ask without looking directly at anyone. "As if I left you?"

"My darling, we all expected it at some point," Mother whispers. "Just not nearly so soon."

Not what I want to hear. I look at Mother and ask, "Expected what?" Heat rises from my feet to my neck. I don't want Miss Jellisia Levion to be right.

"Based on what little we understand, you couldn't very well stay with us forever," Father says.

Astrael puts her arm around me. "We know what you are. Mother and Father have always known. When you disappeared that morning, right before, well, you know. When we couldn't find you, that's when they told me."

"I was gathering moss. It was for school." They *knew* about the moss project. I look into my sister's eyes and ask, "Told you what?"

"Yes, my darling," Mother cuts in. "Your father and I knew the moment you opened your eyes for the very first time." Then she looks around before she leans in, "Your eyes. They're amethyst. In our family, babies born with amethyst eyes are, well, they're fairies."

"But you always taught me that fairies don't exist." A lump grows in my throat. Why had they lied to me? "If everyone knows fairies have amethyst eyes, doesn't everyone know I'm a fairy?" I ask.

"Most scraebins don't know anything about fairies," Father says. "And in other families, a fairy would be born with a different feature. A red wart on the left foot, for example."

"Then how do you know? Maybe it's just a myth," I say. My voice cracks. The room feels like it's floating. The walls are too close. My lungs won't fill with air.

"My grandmother's great aunt is a fairy," Mother admits. "When I was a young girl, my mother told me all about her. You see, sometimes, families who have fairies in their bloodline secretly pass along the information from parent to child. While fairies are rare, my grandmother always said a parent must be prepared if there is a possibility her child could be one."

"And in our family, they always have amethyst eyes?" I ask.

"Yes. At least, that's what I was told," Mother replies. "But no one else in the colony knows that."

Part of me wants to believe Miss Jellisia Levion is lonely and odd. And that Mrs. Mildred Erdos is old and confused. But now, with what my parents just told me, it could all be true. It could all be real. Fairies are real. I'm a real fairy.

My shock melts into hurt. "So you thought I'd leave you just because you think I'm a fairy?"

"You *are* a fairy," Father corrects.

"You have to leave us at some point," Mother adds. "You'll outlive us and all those you know. And if others in the colony believe we think you're a fairy, they'll want you to . . ." Mother pauses and looks at Father.

"Leave," Father continues for her. "They'll want you to leave. They won't understand. I've thought about your condition a lot over the years."

Condition? What does Father mean by that?

He goes on, "It'd be much easier for fairies to cut ties before they start losing relatives."

Mother nods in agreement. "We thought maybe you were contacted by another fairy—maybe my great, great, great aunt—and decided to go ahead and leave us."

Tears spill down my face. Miss Jellisia Levion was right. I'm an emotional scraebin. Or fairy. How could my family ever think I'd want to leave them?

"Not that you'd want to." Astrael hugs me close. "But you'll need to leave . . ." She hangs her head and adds, "someday."

"So everything Miss Jellisia Levion said was true?" I bury my face in my hands.

"Who is Miss Jellisia Levion?" Astrael asks.

"A fairy. My mentor." I sob.

"It's okay, Zahra. You don't have to leave just yet," Astrael whispers in my ear.

"You can't leave just yet," Father says. "There's a cat at the bottom of this tree."

I wipe my face and crawl over to the opening of the knothole. "It's fine. That's Gigesdi."

"What's a gigesdi?" Astrael's behind me, peering down at the cat.

"She's a baby cat. Gigesdi is her name. She's my heart animal. One of them. I think I'm supposed to have more."

"Heart animal? A cat?" Father questions from behind Astrael.

"Yes. She already saved my life in the yard behind the birdhouse and in the woods near the construction. And she helped me escape when I was trapped inside Mrs. Mildred Erdos' house. That's when she led me to you."

"Come away from there, all of you," Mother says as she pulls us back inside.

My parents and sister live near the entrance of the knothole. Two other families live above the knothole, and an older screabin lives in the space below it. Since everyone has to pass by my family's home to go outside, Father built a thick door out of bark and ivy for privacy. He closes it behind him.

"Now, how did you come to be trapped in the house? Mildred takes good care of us all. Surely if you told her you were there, she would've let you out," Father says.

Did I hear Father correctly? "Do you mean Mrs. Mildred Erdos?"

"Yes, of course," Mother answers.

My throat tightens. "But she's the one who wouldn't let me out," I squeak out. "She locked all the windows and doors."

Father shakes his head. "That can't be true. She's a member

of the Society of the Sentinelia," he says to Mother.

"But it *is* true!" I insist through tears. "She was the one who found me and brought me to the Robins' house in her backyard. She didn't want me to be friends with Danni. She kidnapped me!"

"Settle down, Zahra," Mother says with her hands on my shoulders. "You've been through a lot. You're not thinking clearly."

"Who's Danni?" Astrael asks.

I pull away from my mother. "She's my best friend," I answer. Then I look only at Astrael. "And she's probably wondering where I am. I was supposed to report back to her more than a day ago. That was the plan. But Mrs. Mildred Erdos wouldn't let me leave. She even gave me clothes to wear. And she had all those magnolia blossoms so I couldn't find you!"

"Please stop, now. Calm yourself." Mother's voice used to make me feel better. Now it upsets me. "It's too early for magnolia blossoms. Are you feeling well?"

"Is Danni another lost scraebin?" Father asks, ignoring Mother's question.

"No—"

"Calmly," Mother repeats.

I take a breath and settle my thoughts. "Danni is human. She's my age. She lives next door to Mrs. Mildred Erdos."

"Well, that explains it," Father declares. "Mildred just wanted to protect you. You can't trust humans who are not part of the Society."

"I think if you knew her, you'd feel differently," I say with my teeth clenched together.

"Tell us about the robins," Mother changes the subject.

After telling them about the birds that took care of me, the

159

nest where I slept, and my attic observatory, Mother decides it's time for dandelion tea. Father gets the tea. Mother sits next to me. "Now, tell me, my beautiful daughter, what do you know of being a fairy. How long have you known this Miss Jellisia Levion? And what has she told you?"

My puffy eyes are heavy by the time I finish describing the day I spent with my mentor. That's when Mother says we've all had enough. She tucks me in next to my sister.

My heart is full. But also heavy. Confused. Sad.

35

ASTRAEL MEETS DANNI

"Mrs. Erdos!" Danni yells, banging her fist on the front door of the log cabin. "Please, Mrs. Erdos. It's Danni."

Astrael and I are on our bellies, hiding and peeking from the knothole.

"Is that your human friend?" Astrael whispers.

"Yes. But she's supposed to be grounded. She's not allowed to be here."

The door opens. Danni hurls questions at Mrs. Mildred Erdos right through big, fat tears. "She never came back, Mrs. Erdos! Do you know where Zahra is? Was that boy next door outside playing? Has she come here? Mrs. Erdos, I'm scared. What if she got hurt and needs us? Please, you have to help. Please. We have to find her!"

Mrs. Mildred Erdos puts her hand on Danni's shoulder. "Young lady, calm down." She pulls a cloth handkerchief from one of her pockets.

After wiping her face and spectacles and blowing her nose, Danni asks again, "Is she here?"

"Yes, Danni. She's here . . . somewhere." She looks around. "She's been staying with me."

"She has?" Danni cocks her head and tries to look into the house.

Mrs. Mildred Erdos leans to one side and blocks Danni's view. "Is that so hard to believe? It's my job. I protect innocent scraebins from humans like you."

Danni hangs her head. Then she wipes her nose once more. "Can you please tell her I miss her? And I hope she finds her family?"

"If it comes up. Now get yourself home before I call your parents." Mrs. Mildred Erdos slams the door. Danni stands there and looks at her feet. She sniffles.

Astrael sits up and whispers into my ear, "But you're not there. That Sentinelian lady lied to your friend."

"I'm going to go down and talk to her," I announce.

Astrael grabs my arm. "No, you can't go down there now."

I turn and look at my sister. "Why not?"

"What if that old lady human sees you? She might snatch you and lock you back in the house."

She's right. We decide to wait until Danni gets back home. Then I can fly over for a visit. Astrael asks if she can come with me. My heart warms at the thought of introducing my sister to my best friend. I wrap my arms around her.

We wait for the shadow of the magnolia tree to reach past the mossy pointed rock near the stream. Then we fly high over Mrs. Mildred Erdos' house. When we fly over the birdhouse, I feel bad for not letting the Robins know I'm safe. I decide we need to see the Robins after our visit with Danni. We land on the window ledge outside Danni's room.

"Zahra! You're okay!" Danni yelps as she pushes up her

window. With a quieter voice, she asks, "Who is this? Is she from Mrs. Erdos' house?"

"Hi Danni! I'd like you to meet my sister, Astrael."

Danni's hand flies over her mouth and her eyebrows shoot up. She blurts out, "You found your sister!"

"Yes, and Mother and Father, too."

"Oh Zahra, that's wonderful!" Danni turns to my sister, "Hello, Astrael. I'm Danni."

"Hello, Danni. I, I—" Astrael tries to answer.

"My sister is scared. She's never spoken to a human. Not even to a Sentinelian," I explain.

"I would never hurt either one of you, Astrael. Come in, please," Danni waves her hand, inviting us inside. "Sit down. I want to hear about how Mrs. Erdos found your family for you. And I thought you were there because she was keeping you away from me."

"She was, Danni," I blurt out. "That's *exactly* what she was doing. She had me locked up in her house. And all along, she knew my family and others from our colony were in the magnolia tree growing through her front porch." I tell Danni about being captured and how Gigesdi led me out past the wall of magnolia blossoms. And how as soon as I was past the blossoms, I knew my family was only steps away. Astrael is too nervous to say anything, but she listens to every word, just like Danni.

"That's terrible! She's supposed to protect scraebins, not separate their families. We need to find out why Mrs. Mildred Erdos did this to you," Danni says. "You should tell your parents everything. Maybe they can help."

"But she did tell our parents," Astrael finally says. Danni and I both look at her. "They believe Mrs. Mildred Erdos was protecting her from you, not kidnapping her."

"A child's word against an adult's word—and they think Mrs. Erdos is a trusted adult." Danni thinks for a moment. "Then it's up to me," she announces and crosses her arms.

"You?" I ask. "What can you do? Aren't you still grounded?"

"Yes, but on my way home from school, I can stop next door again. Only this time . . ." Danni grabs her notepad and a pencil.

I turn to my sister, "She's good at coming up with plans. And she likes to write stuff on her notepad."

"Okay, I'll work on what I'm going to say. What I need you two to do is have your parents watching from the tree when Mrs. Erdos opens the door."

"You mean *if* she opens the door," Astrael corrects.

Danni looks up at Astrael. "If?"

"Well, yes. She closed the door on you, today. She wasn't friendly. What if she doesn't open the door when she sees it's you again?"

"Your sister makes a good point, Zahra. I need a backup plan in case she doesn't open the door." Danni taps her pencil on the notepad.

We all take a moment to think.

"Cookies," I say.

"Cookies?" Astrael questions.

"Of course! Cookies. She especially liked my mom's snickerdoodles last time. We have more in the freezer. I'll put a bag of them in my backpack tonight. She'll definitely open the door if she sees I have more cookies."

It's a great plan. Before we leave, I tell Astrael I want to stop by the Robins' house on the way home.

"Please don't do that," Danni begs. "Mrs. Erdos can see the

birdhouse. She'll see you if you stop."

Danni's right. Until we know what Mrs. Mildred Erdos is up to, I don't want her to see me. She doesn't know I'm with my family. And in the pit of my stomach and with every piece of my heart, I'm sure I don't want her to know.

Astrael and I fly nearly as high as the treetops on our way back home. The sun is low. The shadows stretch enough to cover most of the ground. We've been away too long.

We climb into the knothole.

Father is waiting for us.

"I don't know where you two have been, but I do know you're not going anywhere anytime soon. Get inside and apologize to your mother. She's been pacing and fretting all afternoon."

"Oh but Father, we need to—" I try to explain.

"You need to go inside. Now!" he demands.

36

SISTER TIME

"What are we going to do now, Zahra?" Astrael asks. "Danni will be at Mrs. Mildred Erdos' door after school tomorrow, and Father won't listen to us."

Father not only sent us to our room, but he's also guarding the doorway. When he needs to step away, he asks Mother to watch us. We aren't sure how long we'll be grounded. Our plan will be ruined if our parents don't watch Danni stop by Mrs. Mildred Erdos' house.

"Maybe he just needs time," I say. "Tomorrow morning, when he's rested, we can talk to him."

"That's a good idea," Astrael agrees. "After a good night's sleep, I'm sure he'll listen to us."

I'm glad Astrael thinks so. Father didn't let us speak when he was scolding us. I've never seen his face look so wrinkled and green.

"Are you afraid of being a fairy?" Astrael surprises me with the question.

"Afraid? Why would I be afraid?"

"It must be a big responsibility. Mother told me fairies have important jobs. And I've heard that you'll live much longer than any of us. Won't you be lonely after we all die?"

My stomach tightens at the thought. "I'll be sad. But let's not talk about that. I'm so happy to be with you now."

"But won't you have to leave soon?" she asks. Her eyes move between the door and me. "Haven't you already met your mentor?"

"Yes, but I think I get to decide when it's best to leave." That's how I hope it works. And considering my age, Miss Jellisia Levion should let me live with my family for another 50 or 60 years.

"Tell me about your heart animal, that scary cat." Astrael's eyes grow big as she waits for me to explain. Unlike most scraebins, she acts excited about the whole fairy thing.

"I was afraid of Gigesdi when I first saw her. But Danni wasn't. She fed her." I pause. Astrael stares at me without blinking. "I didn't think that was a good idea. I wanted the cat to go away. But it never did. Instead, Gigesdi began showing up when I needed help. She saved my life more than once."

"Tell me more about heart animals," Astrael says.

"I think heart animals are like a fairy's team. They protect, comfort, help . . ." I shrug my shoulders, "and become the fairy's family, I suppose." I'm not sure about any of this.

Astrael scoots closer. "Do you have more heart animals?"

"I will. But Miss Jellisia Levion said they might not all be born, yet."

"How many? Do you know how many you'll have?" A pile of questions sit just behind Astrael's eyes, which now shift back and forth between my eyes.

"According to the rocks," I continue, "there will be seven."

"The rocks? What does that mean? Oh, this is so wonderful!

No wonder you're not afraid. I bet your heart animals will live as long as you do." Astrael's excitement reminds me of Danni. I giggle.

"Miss Jellisia Levion saw rocks that matched the color of my eyes. She said the number of rocks she counted is the number of heart animals I'll have."

"I'm so proud to be your sister, Zahra. I hope you'll stay with us for our whole lives. Mother said fairies leave their families when they find out they're fairies. But you came back this time, so maybe you won't leave. You won't leave, will you?" Her face is so close I can feel the warmth of her nose.

"I'd love to stay with you. I want to go back to school, too."

Astrael's smile disappears. She settles back on her knees and hangs her head. "Miss Evelie Poeley left with the others. We don't have a teacher in our colony anymore."

We sit in silence.

I love Miss Evelie Poeley. She's smart and nice. She always made us feel like we could know everything. She wanted us to share what we learned with all our friends and neighbors. She made learning fun.

After a deep breath, I listen to the sounds of the tree trunk. It moves slowly as its branches sway with the wind. It groans like an old toad that's tired and hungry.

"We'll just learn from our parents," Astrael says. "That's how scraebins were taught for generations. We were fortunate to have Miss Evelie Poeley. I remember Mother saying very few colonies have teachers."

"I always thought she said that so we'd get ready faster in the morning." We both smile.

Then Astrael whispers, "Do you think our parents know enough to teach us?"

We laugh so loudly we get Father's attention. "If you're enjoying your punishment so much, I can separate you," he barks.

We cover our mouths. We know he'll never separate us. He's stern, but softhearted. He doesn't want us to be alone. And, he can't guard two doorways at once.

"I think you'll make a wonderful fairy," Astrael whispers.

"Thank you. I wish you could be a fairy, too." I really do wish that. And Danni, too. Then we could all be together for hundreds of years.

"I think one fairy in the family is quite enough," Astrael says. "It's going to be hard, you know?"

"What is?" I ask.

"Staying with us, knowing you're a fairy. No one else can know. They'd be awful to you. Most scraebins think fairies are—"

"I know," I cut her off. The horrible things we were taught to think about scraebins who think they are fairies has been upsetting me since I met Miss Jellisia Levion. "No one can know but you, Mother, and Father."

"How will you explain going away for moons at a time?"

"Going away?" I ask.

"Yes. I'm sure you'll have to meet with your mentor. I suppose we could say you're visiting a relative in another colony. Or searching for a better place for us all to move. We can come up with something."

I hadn't thought about meeting with Miss Jellisia Levion or my family lying to protect me. It doesn't feel right. The others will catch on one day. Once they do, they'll kick me out of the colony. They might also be unkind to my family. "Let's not think about that now," I say. "We need to concentrate on what we're going to say to Father in the morning. He and Mother must watch Danni when she visits Mrs. Mildred Erdos after school."

"We'll just tell him the truth," Astrael says sternly. "He'll understand. And we'll promise to stay in our room the whole time. That way he'll know we are taking our punishment seriously."

Astrael's positive spirit makes me feel better. I love being with my sister again, which makes it even more difficult to think about leaving her for good one day.

37

DANNI AT THE DOOR

A s soon as Astrael and I finish cleaning the breakfast dishes, we tell Father everything. He quietly listens. When we're done with our story, he tells us to sit and listen to him.

"Maybe fairies have human friends, but scraebins do not. Zahra, I'm disappointed in you for putting your sister in danger. That's all I have to say about it. Your mother will be sitting at your door this afternoon. I have to collect dandelions, berries, and seeds."

My cheeks turn hot. Father is disappointed. Maybe he's ashamed his younger daughter is a fairy.

"It sounds as if Mother and Father are planning a delicious stew," Astrael says. She puts her hand on my shoulder. She whispers in my ear, "Please don't worry about what Father said. He doesn't understand, but he will. He just needs a little more time."

It's nice my sister believes in me, but we don't have time. Danni is stopping by Mrs. Mildred Erdos' house today. Father needs to believe before this afternoon.

I try to think of something to say that will change Father's heart. Nothing comes to mind. The way he looks at us tells me he doesn't want me to speak. What he wants is for Astrael and me to go to our room. I hang my head and follow Astrael out of the kitchen.

We spend the day weaving. Mother sits near the door to our room showing us how to blend fibers to make designs. Mine looks like an old bird's nest that was squashed by a human's car. Instead of paying attention to Mother, all I can think about is Danni.

After a while, Mother puts her weaving down and lifts my chin with her hand. "You know Zahra, we're very happy to have you home again. We've missed you so much."

"Thank you, Mother. I'm happy to be home," I answer without looking up.

"You don't look happy."

"I'm ashamed that I disappointed Father," I tell her.

"Oh, nonsense. He's not disappointed," Mother replies.

I look up at her, "But he said—"

"I know what he said," Mother cuts in. "But I promise you, he's not disappointed. He's just a little confused. And scared."

"Scared? Father?" I ask. Scary sometimes when he raises his voice. But not scared.

Astrael puts her weaving down and moves closer to me.

"He's so proud of both of you. And he's had a long time to adjust to you being a fairy, Zahra. Like I said, we've known since you were born. At first, he was devastated. But your bright and adventurous personality won over his heart." Mother looks down at her hands, and then continues, "He was devastated again when we lost you. He couldn't believe that you'd left so early. He expected you to grow up and be part of our family until you were much older. Maybe even until we passed on." I take a deep breath. We all do. "Then, when you returned," Mother looks directly into my eyes, "he was so happy. But he also dreads having to lose you all over again. He loves you deeply, my sweet Zahra. And so do I."

I shake my head and ask, "Then why doesn't he believe me about Mrs. Mildred Erdos?"

"He doesn't want to."

"But, Mother," Astrael begins. "He must. Poor Zahra was kidnapped. She'd still be there if not for her heart cat."

"I think he's trying to understand," Mother says.

"What makes you say that?" I ask.

"Because he's at the entrance of the knothole awaiting your friend Danni's visit."

Relief and happiness fill my heart. A wide grin spreads across my face. Astrael claps.

"Get back to your weaving and hush," Mother says. She's smiling, too. "You're not supposed to know what your father is up to."

We pick up our weaving tools, but it's hard to work after what Mother said.

That evening at supper, Father announces we're no longer grounded. Then he tells us about Danni's visit. He says that when Mrs. Mildred Erdos answered the door, Danni held out the cookies and thanked her for letting Zahra go home. Mrs. Mildred Erdos didn't take the bag of snickerdoodles. Instead, she got upset and asked Danni why she thought Zahra was home. Danni said she'd seen her at the birdhouse. Mrs. Mildred Erdos yelled to the sky with a fist in the air, "That's impossible! How could this be, Herbert?" Then, she slammed the door.

Father says that's when he flew over the house to see if Mrs. Mildred Erdos was going to check the birdhouse. By the time he was above her house, she was running out her back door. Danni ran around the house so she could watch from her backyard. The bag of cookies was still in her hand. He describes how Mrs. Mildred Erdos screamed at the birdhouse for Zahra to come out. She wanted to know how I escaped. She was crying and yelling that everything was all wrong. Her plan was ruined.

"She kept yelling to Herbert, as if someone named Herbert was actually there with her," Father says. "But she was alone. Then, she collapsed on the steps of her back porch and wept."

"So, she did capture Zahra. She did keep her locked in her house. Everything Zahra told us was true," Mother says.

"I'm sorry I didn't believe you," Father admits to me.

I put my hand on his. "It's okay, I understand."

"But what do we do, now?" Astrael asks.

"Danni is the closest person we have to a Sentinelian who would have our best interests at heart. She's proven that today," Mother says.

"I agree. But she's not a Sentinelian. There is another, an experienced Sentinelian, who lives nearby. We need to consult her," Father states.

"Who?" Astrael asks.

"Clara!" I shout.

"Zahra!" Mother yelps. "That's not how you address an elder. You'll use her title and full name, please."

"I'm sorry," I tuck my chin, embarrassed. "Mrs. Clara Festmire."

"And how do you know of her?" Father asks with a raised eyebrow.

My head drops even lower. "I was spying on Mrs. Mildred Erdos one day, and Mrs. Clara Festmire stopped by for a visit."

"Spying?" Father questions. His face flushes green.

"Yes. But I didn't know she was a Sentinelian. I was trying to find out who put the sappy log into the birdhouse for me."

"So, she *was* helping you?" Father asks.

"Only because she'd put me in the birdhouse with the Robins, which made me sick. I needed to be in a tree. With my family. But she kept me from you." Anger shoots up from my belly. My face feels greener than Father's.

Mother puts an arm around me. "She sounds like a tortured soul. Confused. I'm sure she had her reasons for doing what she did," Mother says. "I'm sure she meant no real harm."

"Mother! She let Zahra get sick," Astrael snaps. "What if she'd died?"

"She put the stick in the birdhouse. She meant no lasting harm. She's a Sentinelian, after all. I'm sure Mrs. Festmire can help us. Your father and I will go visit her tomorrow. The two of you can visit Danni and thank her."

"Really?" I ask, shocked that my mother would make the suggestion.

Mother looks at Father.

"Yes," Father agrees.

"Wait!" A much better idea pops into my head. "May we all meet with Mrs. Clara Festmire? And then together, as a family, visit Danni? I would love for you to meet her."

Mother looks at Father again. This time, there's no smile. Instead, her eyebrows are crumpled together.

"Children are not supposed to meet with Sentinelia, but I believe we can make an exception considering the circumstances. And I would very much like to meet Danni. Wouldn't you, dear?"

Mother nods, but her face is still scrunched.

38

MRS. CLARA FESTMIRE

W e eat a large breakfast and pack snacks and water. It's going to be a long day. First, we fly to Mrs. Clara Festmire's house. It's nearly as far as the forest Danni and I visited, but we're not on a bicycle hiding in a backpack. Instead, we fly from treetop to treetop.

Mrs. Clara Festmire's house is quiet when we arrive. We hoped she'd be home. She's not. Father finds a tree that overlooks her front porch. He and Mother decide we'll stay here and rest. And wait.

"What if she went on a journey? She may not come home for days," Astrael says. "Why don't we go see Danni?" Meeting a Sentinelian is scary for Astrael, especially after the stories about Mrs. Mildred Erdos.

"She can't be far," Father tells us. "Sentinelia stay near their homes. When they leave, it's only for short periods of time. It's part of their code."

"Is that her?" Mother points to a lady walking toward us. She's wearing a wide-brimmed straw hat trimmed with wildflowers.

"That's her," I announce.

We huddle close and watch. Mrs. Clara Festmire walks to her front door. She unlocks it and stops. Then she turns and looks up into the tree.

"Come in, won't you? I've been expecting you," she says. She turns around to open the door.

As soon as we fly inside, we see scraebin-sized furniture arranged on her living room coffee table. It reminds me of how Mrs. Mildred Erdos set up furniture on her coffee table, but this furniture looks more like what we'd have in our knotholes. And there are four chairs, as if Mrs. Clara Festmire really *did* know we were coming to visit.

"I've got tea ready. Just give me a moment." She goes into her kitchen and then returns with tea in acorn caps and a stone plate filled with seeds.

"Hello, Mrs. Festmire. I'm Berniad Aylward. And this is my wife Landrea, and our daughters, Astrael and Zahra." He points to us.

"And as you know, I'm Clara Festmire."

"Yes, but if I may ask, how did you know we would visit?" Father asks.

"A Sentinelian knows." She smiles. Then she adds, "The strange phone call I received yesterday evening from Mildred served as a heads up, as well. I've been worried about her—and all of you—for quite some time."

Mrs. Clara Festmire tells us that Mrs. Mildred Erdos is much older than we thought. She hasn't had any scraebins in her care for many years. Not since her husband, Mr. Herbert Erdos, passed away. When she found my family and the others from our colony, she decided to care for them. But then she found me.

"Astrael, are you alright?" I whisper.

"She's . . . so . . . big," she whispers back without taking her eyes off Mrs. Clara Festmire.

I put my hand in hers. "She is, but her heart is kind."

"But . . . Mrs. Mildred Erdos . . . she captured you."

She makes an excellent point. I glance at the window near the front door. It's open. Mrs. Clara Festmire stops her story and looks at me, "Children, my windows are always open when I entertain scraebins. You should always have a way out and never feel captive."

My sister squeezes my hand.

Mrs. Clara Festmire goes on with her story. She describes Mrs. Mildred Erdos as a sad, lonely person who wants only to make sure scraebins will be able to survive once she's gone, despite the increase in human population and the construction that's destroying our homes.

"But how was she going to save us?" Father asks.

"Our special one, Zahra." Mrs. Clara Festmire looks at me again. Then she continues, "She was an experiment. Mildred wanted to find a way for scraebins to live outside of trees."

She tells us that Mrs. Mildred Erdos thought scraebins needed to adapt to live in little houses, like the ones made for birds. Finding large trees near Sentinelia is getting harder with each passing year.

"Mildred thought living in a birdhouse and sleeping on a nest of fresh twigs with the occasional sappy stick placed inside would be enough," Mrs. Clara Festmire explains. "Eventually, she thought scraebins would evolve to be less dependent on tree sap."

"But it wasn't enough," I say.

"No, it wasn't. Not even for a fairy," she replies.

"You know our Zahra is a fairy?" Mother questions.

Mrs. Clara Festmire nods.

"How?" I ask.

"Jellisia Levion was one of my charges well before she knew she was a fairy."

"That's not possible," I say. If what I learned is right, Mrs. Clara Festmire's story can't be true. "Miss Jellisia Levion is much older than you."

"You have so much to learn, young Zahra." Mrs. Clara Festmire says.

"Didn't Mrs. Erdos know that Zahra was becoming ill from living outside of a tree?" Mother asks, getting us back to the story.

"She did. I believe that's why she took her into her house. She wanted Zahra to get well, and she needed to re-group. She needed a new plan. A new test for Zahra. Although, I wasn't able to glean what that would have been. Instead, Zahra escaped, thanks to a heart animal, I'm sure."

I nod. "Gigesdi, my cat."

"Well, she was in quite a state after your friend Danishia suggested you'd gone back to the birdhouse. The father robin had to peck her head to keep her from disturbing the nest. Those robins have eggs they're working to hatch. Mildred's tirade was quite upsetting to them."

My heart sinks at the thought of anything happening to Mr. and Mrs. Robin and their eggs.

"We must all move from the tree on her front porch," Father says.

I look at him but don't know what to say. We can't move too far. I want to be near Danni. She's my best friend.

"That would be wise," Mrs. Clara Festmire agrees. "Although,

I do believe you should be near a Sentinelian. I worry about those who relocated west of here. It was a long and dangerous journey for them. There are only two Sentinelia between here and the Blue Ridge Mountains."

"Well, I don't think we need to travel quite so far," Mother says.

A sigh of relief pushes out of my nose. I look at Father, hoping he agrees.

"We don't need to stay here," Father says. "There's too much construction."

"What about your yard? You have trees on your property," Astrael suggests.

I'm proud of her for speaking up, especially since she's so nervous being in a human's house. And it's a great idea. Danni could easily ride her bike here.

Mrs. Clara Festmire takes a sip of her tea. "That's a commitment I don't believe I can make. I certainly don't want to end up like Mildred, losing my wits and breaking rules—even if her heart meant no real harm."

"Are there other Sentinelia nearby?" Mother asks.

"Not in this neighborhood. We have a small group from this region that meets on Birkhead Mountain. Many are older, though, like me. At our society meeting last Tuesday, we meditated on the possibility of new Sentinelia. After quiet time on the ridge where we meet, sitting among fresh buds poking from the tree limbs, we felt the faint presence of just one. But we all felt strongly the person is too young to display all the characteristics. There's no way, yet, to identify and evaluate them. It could be many years before we take on this potential new Sentinelian."

Maybe Mrs. Clara Festmire and her Tuesday group don't

know who the young Sentinelian is, but my heart knew exactly who it *had* to be.

39

DANNI MEETS THE FAMILY

anni can't stop grinning after I introduce her to my parents. Astrael's not as nervous this time, but my parents look terrified. Father stands between Danni and all of us with his chest pushed out. Mother is smoothing her skirt and darting her eyes between Danni, Father, Astrael, and me.

Father begins by thanking Danni. Mother repeats his words. Danni's neck and face turn bright pink. She leaves her room to find snacks. She returns with a saucer of cookie pieces. Some are peanut butter, but some are snickerdoodles—my favorite! After my family enjoys the homemade human sweets, we tell Danni everything Mrs. Clara Festmire told us about Mrs. Mildred Erdos.

"I still don't understand why she had to separate you," Danni says.

"She was strong enough for the experiment. Any of us would have quickly become fatally ill. We would've died," Father explains. "She knew Zahra was a fairy. Zahra is much stronger."

Danni hangs her head, "Now I feel terrible."

"Why?" Astrael asks.

"I brought her snickerdoodles just to upset her. I was mean to an unwell, older lady. She's my neighbor, and I wasn't neighborly. She was trying to do something good, even if she did it all wrong."

"Your intentions were also good," Mother points out.

"And, as a Sentinelian, she knew better," Father adds.

"I still feel terrible," Danni repeats.

"Me too," I agree. "She was so upset. Maybe we should visit her."

"And get caught in her house and used in her experiments?" Mother blurts out—her eyes darting about again. "I understand feeling bad for this human, even remorseful. But that doesn't mean we need to fall prey to her misguided ways."

"But if we all go, Danni, too . . ." Astrael looks up at Danni with a big grin, and then continues, "and we all talk to her, she'll see she was wrong."

"Your heart is generous, Astrael," Father says. "But we need to be cautious. You've been introduced to two very kind humans. It's easy to forget how big and dangerous they can be. We'd have to think this through fully. We'd have to take every precaution."

Memories of being dropped into one of Mrs. Mildred Erdos' pockets and being trapped in her house flash through my mind. Father is right. Down deep, she might be a good human. But, she is, as Mother said, misguided. And she's big.

"Do you think Mrs. Festmire could join us?" Danni asks. Then she pops straight up, startling Mother so much that she falls backward. Father steadies Mother upright, and then puts his arm around her. "I need my notepad and a pencil," Danni announces, never noticing Mother's near fall.

"She's a planner," I explain. "She'll help us think it through, Father." Pride fills my heart as I realize she and Father share something in common. No wonder I like her.

"Planning is good," he says. "Your friend is smart, Zahra."

"Yes, she is," I reply with a nod.

We work together on a safe plan. Instead of going to visit Mrs. Mildred Erdos, we decide to attend the Tuesday meeting of the Society of the Sentinelia. Mrs. Clara Festmire is included in our plan. Danni's notepad is filled by the time we hear Danni's parents return from work.

We thank her and say goodbye. Then we fly back home. We're careful to stay high and out of sight of humans—especially Mrs. Mildred Erdos. When I see the birdhouse, guilt nips at my heart. I look around for Mr. Robin. All is quiet. He's not outside gathering berries or worms. Thoughts of what could've happened to the Robins when Mrs. Mildred Erdos was yelling and screaming make my heart race. Then I remember Miss Jellisia Levion.

I suck in a big breath of fresh air. It's sweeter at the treetops, where pale green leaves move with the wind. Sad and scary thoughts leave with each exhale. As soon as we get back to the tree on the front side of Mrs. Mildred Erdos' house, I know in my heart the Robins are fine. But I do miss them.

It's been a big day, so we all take time to rest. All but Father. He goes outside to gather food for supper. When he returns, Astrael and I are asleep. We awake to the sounds of chatter and giggles. He and Mother are preparing a family favorite—blackberry pecan stew. Our home sounds and smells as comfortable as the blanket Mrs. Robin made. It's wonderful to be with my family. I don't ever want to leave them. I want to feel like this forever.

"Where did you find the blackberries?" Astrael asks as she hurries to the table.

"They were piled on a branch just outside our knothole," Father tells her. "They were freshly picked and stacked. Next to the pile was your cloak."

"My cloak!" she squeals. "Oh, Father, where is it?" He points to the corner of the room where it's folded on a rock. Astrael runs over, scoops it up, and wraps it around her. "What happened next, Father?" She asks.

"I stepped closer to pick up the cloak. That's when I saw a calm and fearless robin watching me. It nudged the berries in my direction, as if it were offering them to me. When I picked them up, the robin looked at me, bowed its head, and then flew away."

Mr. Robin! It had to be him. He must know I'm here. My heart flips with joy at the thought the Robins know I'm home safe with my family. They're still taking care of me even though they'll soon have babies of their own.

40

THE TUESDAY MEETING

Mrs. Clara Festmire arrives at the Tuesday meeting of the Society of the Sentinelia with Mrs. Mildred Erdos. She made sure Mrs. Mildred Erdos would attend by stopping at her house and walking with her. Danni is also with them. She scurries over to the tree branch where my family is seated.

For most humans like Danni, it's quite a hike to get to the rock formation on the ridge of the Birkhead Mountain Trail. Sentinelia come here all the time. They climb the trail as if they're butterflies floating over a meadow.

Danni, who's still huffing and puffing, shouldn't have been allowed to attend. It's a school day, and she's still grounded. But her plan for convincing her parents worked. She told them Mrs. Mildred Erdos and her friend, Mrs. Clara Festmire, invited her to go on a hike. Mrs. Clara Festmire then called Danni's parents and let them know she'd heard about Danni being brought home by the deputy officer humans. She said a hike through the forest and time with her elder neighbors would provide Danni with a deeper appreciation and respect for the forest, including its dangers. Danni and Mrs. Clara Festmire left out a few details to protect the Society and scraebins, but what they did tell her parents was true.

Danni's parents went to their room to talk about it. Then they knocked on Danni's door and told her she could go. "After the hike, I have to go straight home and complete the schoolwork I'll miss today," Danni explains. "I also have to write a report about what I learn. Then I have to write notes to the deputies who brought me home. I have to thank them and apologize for being irresponsible."

Father hushes us.

"Tell me again before we begin, why did this child and a group of scraebins need to be present at today's meeting?" a lady wearing a green skirt with leaves and a sweater with white, violet, and yellow flower petals—Mrs. Leaves and Petals Lady—asks.

The humans get quiet.

"It wasn't my idea, was it Herbert?" Mrs. Mildred Erdos says.

Mrs. Clara Festmire speaks up, "Whenever we challenge the behavior of a Sentinelian, we are required to do three things. First, we must reference Book Seven of the Society Tomes, which lists the rules that govern our work. Secondly, we must bring evidence to support our claims. Thirdly, we must offer a solution to the root problem."

One of the gentlemen in the group asks, "So, you mean to challenge the behavior of one of us?" He rubs his silvery chin hairs and looks at Mrs. Clara Festmire.

"Yes, Mr. Cavers, I do."

"There hasn't been a challenge in . . ." Mrs. Leaves and Petals Lady flips through a thick book bound with dried ivy vines.

She then continues, "two hundred twenty-two years."

"Well, we'll have to review the process first then, won't we?" the gentleman wearing a brown jacket with large wooden buttons says.

"I move we do just that," says the smallest lady in the group as she points a finger up at the treetops. Then she puts both hands on the black handles of her green purse.

"Second," adds a gentleman with long dark hair and a turned up mustache.

Mrs. Leaves and Petals Lady pulls out another book and reads. The others listen and nod. Mrs. Mildred Erdos stares at her feet. A teardrop lit by a ray of sun that found its way between the tree branches slides down her cheek.

"I feel so bad for her," Danni whispers to me as she watches Mrs. Mildred Erdos.

"I'm sure they'll be nice to her," I say. "But Father explained to me last night that there needs to be a consequence."

"Consequence?" Danni asks.

"Like when you were grounded. You did something wrong, and your parents punished you. Or when lots of trees are cut down, then the air isn't as fresh, homes are lost, and animals and scraebins—and even humans—suffer. There are always consequences." My explanation isn't as good as Father's, but Danni nods.

"Mrs. Festmire, please state your challenge," Mrs. Leaves and Petals Lady says.

Mrs. Clara Festmire tells the other humans that Mrs. Mildred Erdos broke rule number twelve point thirty-four by experimenting with a scraebin without consent. Father leans next to my ear and explains that she never told me what she was doing. She didn't ask my permission.

189

"This is a very serious challenge, Mrs. Erdos. What's your response?" Mrs. Leaves and Petals Lady asks.

"What are we going to do when there aren't enough trees for the screabins? We already don't have enough Sentinelia to watch over them all, do we, Herbert?"

My eyes follow Mrs. Mildred Erdos' gaze to a squirrel wringing its paws at the edge of a limb well above our heads.

"Mrs. Festmire, please introduce your guests," Mrs. Leaves and Petals Lady says.

Mrs. Clara Festmire introduces Danni, my family, and me. One by one, we share our stories. I tell them everything that happened, from the pieces of memory I have of the day Mrs. Mildred Erdos found me right up to today.

Mrs. Leaves and Petals Lady again asks Mrs. Mildred Erdos to respond.

"I'm quite tired," she says. "I believe I'll take a long nap when I get back home."

"What is your suggested solution to this situation, Mrs. Festmire?" Mrs. Leaves and Petals Lady asks Mrs. Clara Festmire. "And please keep in mind that Zahra is a fairy." She looks directly at me.

How does everyone know that about me?

"Mildred served the screabins well for many years," begins Mrs. Clara Festmire. "She and her husband Herbert were two of the best among us. When he passed on, it shattered her heart. She was devastated. It was that great loss, I believe, that altered her judgment. I don't doubt she always had the well-being of screabins driving her actions.

"Many of you, like Mildred and I, have been around long enough to see the destruction of many of the Earth's resources. Deforestation, pollution, urbanization driven by population growth, industrialization, and technology. At the same time, the Society is shrinking. There were no new Sentinelia identified when Herbert passed away. Jack here," she points to the man with long dark hair and a turned up mustache—Mr. Jack Mustache, "was the last one identified in our region. And we've lost two others since then.

"But what she did was detrimental not only to Zahra, but to our mission. We are dedicated to the protection of the scraebin culture and the environment they, and we, need to survive."

Mrs. Leaves and Petals Lady's eyes are slits. Her jaw is tight. "Your recommendation?"

"Of course, my apologies," Mrs. Clara Festmire says. "I recommend that Mildred be officially stripped of her duties, including the revocation of her set of the Society Tomes and any items directly related to the care of scraebins. I further recommend we assign another Sentinelian to watch over her, keep her company, care for her, and ensure she has no further interactions with scraebins."

Humans nod and mumble. "Yes, it's time." "Sounds appropriate."

Mrs. Leaves and Petals Lady asks Mrs. Mildred Erdos again for a response.

Mrs. Mildred Erdos looks at the other members, then at me. She turns to Mrs. Leaves and Petals Lady and says, "I believe it's time for me to withdraw."

Everyone gasps.

41

NEW ASSIGNMENT

Mrs. Leaves and Petals Lady hushes the group. "Let Mildred speak," she demands.

Mrs. Mildred Erdos looks at Mrs. Clara Festmire. Then she stands to talk to the group. "I'm tired. It's time," is all she says.

"So be it. I ask you give us until Saturday to prepare our hearts, Mildred," Mrs. Leaves and Petals Lady says to her. Mrs. Mildred Erdos nods and sits down. Mrs. Leaves and Petals Lady bangs a piece of wood and calls for a break. The humans group together in clusters and whisper.

"What does that mean?" I ask Father.

Danni and Astrael lean closer. "It means she has agreed to let go," Father replies. "Sentinelia live many, many years. Much longer than other humans. When they are ready to die, they withdraw, as she said. They close their eyes, take a last breath, and let go of life. That's how they perish."

Danni's lower lip trembles, "That's terrible! I don't want her to die. Can't we stop her? This is wrong." She starts to cry and shake her head.

"If they didn't let go, they'd just go on living," Father explains.

"That's not true," Danni says in a loud voice. "People live only eighty or ninety years. They get sick or too old and *then* die."

Mrs. Clara Festmire walks over and puts her arms around Danni. "There, there, child. It may shock you to know this, but Mildred is 389 years old. When she became a full member of the Society, she and Herbert were newlyweds living just outside of Liverpool, England."

"But that's impossible," Danni says between sniffles. Her spectacles are dotted with dried tears.

"And not long ago, you didn't know scraebins existed," Mrs. Clara Festmire tells her.

"But how did they end up here if they lived in England?" Danni asks.

My parents, Astrael, and I stare at Mrs. Clara Festmire. We wait for an answer.

She shakes her head. Then she explains, "When word of fighting between Native Americans and Europeans spread to Sentinelia in England, there was a call for some to relocate to America. She and Herbert were among the first to make the move. That's when they built the log cabin. He maintained it all those years. Back then, theirs was the only house at the base of the Uwharrie Mountains. They helped convince the American government to protect much of the land around here." She looks around at the trees and rock formations.

Then she looks at Danni and continues, "When your house and the one on the other side of the cabin where that little boy lives were built, Herbert had had enough. It upset him to see so many trees destroyed. Watching pollution increase hurt his heart. He couldn't plant enough new trees or clean all the litter.

He became frustrated. And tired. So, he let go.

"At first, Mildred was angry at him for leaving her. But then she began coming to our meetings again. She mentored Jack for a while." Mrs. Clara Festmire looks at Mr. Jack Mustache and smiles. "She was consulted on many issues. But the longer she lived without directly caring for scraebins, the more she began to talk to Herbert as if he were still here. That's when she really began to change. Then, right before she found Zahra, when more construction began across the stream, she became angry. And scared. She was convinced that despite many hundreds of years of the dedication and work of the Society of the Sentinelia, we'd all failed the scraebins."

"Have you? Has the Society failed scraebins?" Danni's red eyes stare at Mrs. Clara Festmire.

"Maybe."

Mrs. Leaves and Petals Lady clears her throat. "With the challenge settled, it's time for regular business."

Mrs. Clara Festmire returns to the group. Danni wipes her face and blows her nose with a paper handkerchief. We all stay quiet. Members talk about scraebin colonies they look after as well as what they're doing to help protect trees and forests. One talks about leading groups to clean the rivers and streams. Another speaks about something called recycling. Another tells the group she presented a plan to leaders about increasing the amount of land protected as National Forest.

When it's Mrs. Clara Festmire's turn to give a report, she talks about our colony. "They live in the magnolia on Mildred's front porch. Once Mildred withdraws, the government will likely take the land and destroy the house so two more can be built. We need to move these families as soon as possible. Are there any suggestions?"

"Yes!" Danni's hand flies up.

"Will the group hear from this guest?" Mrs. Leaves and Petals Lady asks. Everyone turns to look at Danni. Then they nod. "Okay, then. Come up here and speak your peace, child."

Danni walks to the front of the group. She wipes her nose before she speaks. "There's a large tree in my backyard. They could move there. I'll watch over them."

"That's a generous offer, child. But you're not at all equipped to watch over scraebins. You're not a Sentinelian," Mrs. Leaves and Petals Lady says to her.

"May I address this idea?" Mrs. Clara Festmire asks. Mrs. Leaves and Petals Lady nods. "We have sensed for some time now that there is a new Sentinelian in the area. We've agreed that while this new one is vaguely in our midst somewhere near the Uwharrie Mountains, this person is still too young for us to identify. It could be years before we find them and begin the evaluation process. We also know that Zahra is a fairy." She waves her hand in my direction. "She's too young to fully enter into mentorship, but she's already proven adept at understanding through her senses. Miss Danni, while still a child, has proven reliable and pure of heart."

"All interesting, Clara," Mrs. Leaves and Petals Lady says. "But please, make your point."

Mrs. Clara Festmire nods. "Of course. I suggest that while we await the revelation of the new Sentinelian, we allow this small colony to relocate to the tree behind Miss Danishia's house. Zahra can help keep them safe. And I'm close enough to assist when needed until we are able to identify the new Sentinelian."

"Thank you, Clara." Mrs. Mildred Erdos whispers without looking at anyone.

Mrs. Leaves and Petals Lady speaks, "Is there a provision in the Society Tomes for such an arrangement?"

Mr. Jack Mustache answers, "If I may?"

"You may," Mrs. Leaves and Petals Lady replies.

"As you all know, I study the Society Tomes daily to ensure I'm acting within the rules governing Sentinelia. Being one of the newest among you, I feel it's best for me—"

"Yes, we're aware of your diligence, Jack," Mrs. Leaves and Petals Lady interrupts. "Now please, go on."

"Yes, ma'am. In Book Seven, Chapter Fifteen, Rule Seven, it states that in a situation in which there are no Sentinelia available for scraebins who do want protection—"

"Rule Seven-Fifteen-Seven! Of course!" yells Mrs. Clara Festmire. Everyone looks at her. "My apologies. Do go on, Jack."

Mr. Jack Mustache looks at Mrs. Clara Festmire. He clears his throat. "Well, if by unanimous agreement, our chapter decides this child is capable of the responsibility, we can have her take the Honor Oath. We then provide her the List of Fifteen, which are, as you all know, the fifteen most important rules of the Society. We must also assign a Sentinelian to oversee her."

"Clara has already volunteered to oversee this arrangement," Mrs. Leaves and Petals Lady points out. "All we need now is unanimous agreement."

As the group talks about the idea, Astrael looks at me and grins. "Will we be able to visit Danni's room, as well?" she quietly asks.

"I'm sure we will, but we'll have to be smart about it," I whisper back.

"We'll discuss that once we're settled," Father says.

"Yes, I'm not sure I like the idea of you two spending time inside a house, even if it is Danni's," Mother agrees.

Mrs. Leaves and Petals Lady asks each member if they're in agreement with using the Rule of Seven-Fifteen-Seven. Everyone responds with "yes." Mrs. Leaves and Petals Lady opens a book and waves to Danni so she'll stand in front of the group. Danni smiles, steps forward, and takes the oath:

"I, Danni Allman, with an open heart and mind;

Amongst the Society of the Sentinelia, do accede;

To do my best to protect, serve, and be kind;

To all scraebins, young and old, and help with any need.

"Amongst other humans, none shall come to light;

Knowledge of scraebins and my earnest pledge to all;

Never loosed from my lips or words I write;

Ensuring scraebin protection. I accept this call."

On the way home, I fly to Mrs. Clara Festmire's shoulder and ask, "Don't you think Danni might be the new Sentinelian?"

Mrs. Clara Festmire smiles. "It's so easy to think any child I meet could be a new Sentinelian. From what I've observed in my many years, children are naturally connected to and respectful of the environment and other creatures."

"Yes but—"

"We won't know who the new Sentinelian is for many years. Whether she is or not, I believe in my heart that she is up for this special task."

Acknowledgements

Our relationships define, lift, encourage, and motivate us. There are so many people I need to acknowledge and thank for helping along the way.

My father, Gary Schramm, instilled in me a love of nature and hunger for hiking—the seeds that sprouted into Zahra's story. He, along with my mother, Ella Schramm, nurtured my love of writing by working with my second grade teacher, Mrs. Ott, to get me a Collegiate Thesaurus. Its worn pages are still cherished.

My children, Elliott Finch, Ethan Finch, and Evan Finch, always believed in my dreams. Their assumption that I'd realize them is still a powerful and driving force on this journey.

My husband, Dave, believes, supports, reads, and is the one who keeps the house in shape, dishes washed, and food made when I have to write, edit, market, and everything else tied to being an author.

My original critique group, Karen Fritz and Lynn Chandler Willis, provided honest, candid feedback despite the fact they write in a different genre for a completely different audience.

Thanks to Aunt Jayne for sharing my manuscript with her Chicago critique group, who collectively provided excellent, candid feedback, as well.

Thanks to my friends and family who answered the call

to help get the word out about my book, author visits, and reviewers, including Teri De Bello-Tahany, Joel & Kristen McClosky, Jaimi Kosa, Vanessa Hernandez, Alex Licht, and Erin Bare.

Thanks to my youth reviewers, Estella McClosky, Cassie & Patti Anderson, and Rebecca Boomer. Your passion for reading and honest perspectives motivate and inspire me.

RhinoLeap Productions, thanks for capturing the spirit of this book in 30 seconds. Thanks also to Sabine Langer and Ella Schramm for starring in the trailer.

To my boss, Lisa Hayworth, and all my work colleagues, thank you for the flexibility to do this while working full time, along with endless support and encouragement.

Thank you Jacquie Reininger for designing my custom signature glasses that perfectly match the tone of the Zahra of the Uwharries series. And thanks to Tim Nelson for working with me on my bookmarks and swag.

And finally, thank you to Shawn Reilly Simmons, my creative and talented editor. Our virtual meeting during the pandemic was the epitome of serendipity. Thank you for your faith in my abilities and the guidance that produced the best version of Zahra's story.

About the Author

Micki Bare is a graduate of N.C. State University. Her career in early childhood spans three decades, with service as a teacher, administrator, and marketing director. She is the author of three early reader children's books, is featured in two anthologies, has articles published in magazines, and wrote a human interest column for 18 years. *Society of the Sentinelia* is her debut middle grade novel and is the first of five in the Zahra of the Uwharries series. She loves to write, garden, cook, and hike. She and her husband reside in Asheboro, NC.

SOCIAL MEDIA HANDLES:
  Twitter: https://twitter.com/TurtleAuthor
  Instagram: @mickibare and @zahra_aylward
  Facebook: https://www.facebook.com/MickiBareAuthor
  https://www.tiktok.com/@inspiredscribe

AUTHOR WEBSITE:
  https://www.mickibareauthor.com/books

CPSIA information can be obtained
at www.ICGtesting.com
Printed in the USA
JSHW041926181022
31825JS00003B/189